The Jerry McNeal Series

Merry Me

(A Paranormal Snapshot)

By Sherry A. Burton

Dorry Press

Also by Sherry A. Burton

The Orphan Train Saga
Discovery (book one)
Shameless (book two)
Treachery (book three)
Guardian (book four)
Loyal (book five)
Patience (book six)
Endurance (book seven)

Orphan Train Extras
Ezra's Story

Jerry McNeal Series (Also in Audio)
Always Faithful (book one)
Ghostly Guidance (book two)
Rambling Spirit (book three)
Chosen Path (book four)
Port Hope (book five)
Cold Case (book six)
Wicked Winds (book seven)
Mystic Angel (book eight)
Uncanny Coincidence (book nine)
Chesapeake Chaos (book ten)
Village Shenanigans (book eleven)
Special Delivery (book twelve)
Spirit of Deadwood (a full-length Jerry McNeal novel, book thirteen)
Star Treatment (book fourteen)
Merry Me (book fifteen)
Hidden Treasures (book sixteen)

The Jerry McNeal Series
Merry Me

By Sherry A. Burton

The Jerry McNeal Series: Merry Me
Copyright 2024

By Sherry A. Burton
Published by Dorry Press
Edited and Formatted by BZHercules.com
Cover by Laura J. Prevost
@laurajprevostphotography
Proofread by Latisha Rich

For more information on the author and her works, please see www.SherryABurton.com

A special thanks to:

I will forever be grateful to my mom, who insisted the dog stay in the series.

To my hubby, thanks for helping me stay in the writing chair.

To my editor, Beth, for allowing me to keep my voice.

To Laura, for EVERYTHING you do to keep me current in both my covers and graphics.

To my beta readers for giving the books an early read.

To my proofreader, Latisha Rich, for the extra set of eyes.

To my fans, for the continued support.

Lastly, to my "writing voices," thank you for all the incredible ideas!

Chapter One

Weapon at the ready, Jerry picked his way through the rubble, his heart racing as he struggled to breathe in the desert heat. He motioned for the team to stay close as he led the unit forward, fighting his senses, which begged him to give the men an order to run in the opposite direction. Not for the first time, he cursed his decision to join the Marines. It wasn't that he had a problem with the Marines, nor did he regret serving his country; it was just that he had the bad luck to know things others did not. Bad things. Things that would make a grown man cry.

As they moved through the war-ravaged alley, his blood pulsed, letting him know something was going to happen. Then again, it didn't take psychic radar to figure out something was going to happen. This was a war zone; something bad always happened.

Only this was different, as the feeling had come on the moment his unit started out. The problem was he didn't know what, when, or where. It was that way most of the time when it came to his feelings, only over here, not knowing was almost always a death sentence.

Jerry stepped around the building, scanning the area for the threat. He saw nothing, but it was there. He could feel it with every beat of his pulse.

Simms, a recent transfer to the unit, flanked his right side using the muzzle of his rifle as a pointer to check each window on the neighboring street. Not seeing anything, the man lowered his gun and turned to say something.

Jerry opened his mouth to warn the man that he still felt the threat, but it was too late. An explosion filled the air as Simms fell to the ground.

Jerry fired in the direction of the threat, then dropped to the ground to check on his brother. Only it wasn't Simms lying on the ground, it was April who lay staring at him as if asking why he'd allowed this to happen to her. She whispered something he couldn't hear. Jerry lowered his head, placing his ear to her mouth.

"Is that why you didn't ask me to marry you on Christmas Day? Because you know you can't protect the ones you love?"

Jerry woke in a panic. Relief washed over him as

he saw April sleeping peacefully at his side. It was a dream, and yet it was all he could do not to take her in his arms just to prove to his heart she was still alive. Instead, he gently placed his hand against her chest, taking comfort in the rise and fall of each breath.

He heard a snort and saw Gunter standing beside the bed. The dog emitted a soft whine and wagged his tail as if to say, *Don't worry. It was only a bad dream.*

Satisfied that April wasn't in any immediate danger, Jerry removed his hand from her bosom and reached to touch the ghostly K-9's fur to further settle his nerves. He lay there for several moments, listening to April's slow, gentle breaths before getting up. Even then, he stood staring down at her for several moments before finally leaving the room and heading downstairs. That Gunter followed him down the stairs let him know there was no immediate danger.

Jerry went to the kitchen, made a pot of coffee, and poured himself a cup while rolling the dream around in his mind. He knew part of it stemmed from the hurt he'd seen in April's eyes when they turned in on Christmas Day, and he'd yet to propose to her. Though she hadn't actually said anything, she'd given him enough hints leading up to the holiday to let him know she'd expected it. He wanted to propose. He even had the ring to make it official, but he'd never found the right time. The next day, though April was outwardly cheerful, he could feel her inner tension over his lack of commitment. That tension caused bigger problems, as now it seemed he needed to come up with something even more elaborate to make up for the disappointment he'd caused. If he'd only put the box under the tree as he'd originally intended, he could have avoided this whole mess and not triggered the recent bout of PTSD that was causing him too many sleepless nights.

"That's all this is, right, boy?" he asked, looking at Gunter lying on the floor with his head resting on his front paws, watching his every move. "PTSD? If there were more to it, I would know, wouldn't I?"

Gunter stared at him as if to say, *You got yourself into this mess, you clean it up.*

"Some help you are," Jerry said, taking a sip from his cup.

Gunter lifted his head and yawned a squeaky yawn, then returned his head to his paws.

Jerry retraced the nightmare, which felt as real as any dream he'd ever had – probably because, aside from the fact it was April lying on the ground, the dream had been a true account of what had happened to Simms and one of the final catalysts that had prevented him from reenlisting when his time was up. It wasn't the first time his feelings had warned him that something would happen, and yet he was powerless to do anything to prevent it.

He looked to the ceiling and thought of April, recalling the dream once more.

He had no doubt he loved her, as his heart ached for her whenever they were apart. Was his love enough to keep her safe? Was it even fair to ask her to share a life with him, knowing full well his job could put her in danger? Even Fred had warned that he and the others didn't wear wedding rings for that very reason. Jerry took his coffee cup and stood peering out into the darkness. "Is that the real reason I haven't asked her to marry me? Because, deep down, I know I won't be able to keep her safe?"

His grandmother's ghostly image appeared just outside the window. "Jerry Carter McNeal, stop that right now!" the spirit said, then disappeared.

Jerry turned from the window and saw his grandmother – or at least her ghostly spirit – sitting at the kitchen table.

Gunter scrambled from the floor and hurried to the woman's side, wiggling his delight as she ran her fingers through his fur. "Okay, that's enough," Granny said, giving the dog one final scratch.

Gunter walked to his original spot and lowered into a crouch. The dog's pointed ears twitched as his deep golden-brown eyes watched the woman.

"Did you get my ring resized?" she asked, then took a sip from a cup that wasn't there a moment before.

Jerry nodded. "I did."

She wagged a finger at him. "Then quit making excuses and ask April to be your bride."

"What if I can't keep her safe?" Jerry asked, voicing his fears out loud.

"You mean, what if she dies?"

Ouch. Why did the woman have to be so direct?

"I always was. Why should I stop just because I'm dead?" she said, reading his mind. "You want to know what'll happen? She'll come back and haunt you for not making an honest woman out of her. In my day, living in sin was frowned upon."

Jerry refreshed his coffee and joined her at the table. "In your day, most things were frowned upon."

"It's three in the morning. Why are you awake?" Granny asked, ignoring the comment.

"Nightmare," Jerry replied, then told her about the dream.

"It's been a while since you had one of your Marine dreams."

"First one since I moved in with April and Max," he agreed.

Granny smiled a wrinkled smile. "That's because they settle you."

Jerry ran his hand over his head. "I'm not feeling very settled at the moment."

"It was just a dream, Jerry," she said softly.

Jerry cocked an eyebrow. "Coming from the

woman who told me a dream is never just a dream."

"True, but I also told you to investigate all possible avenues of the dream's meaning, and yet you jumped straight to it, meaning you're not supposed to marry April. That's not the dream talking. That is your own insecurity."

"I didn't say…"

She cut him off. "No, but you were thinking it before I showed up. You're worried about not being able to protect her, but what if you are the only one who can?"

"What if I'm the one who puts her in harm's way in the first place?" Jerry closed his eyes, recalling the dream. "There was an explosion, and she was on the ground."

"So why do you automatically assume that you're the reason she's in danger?"

"Because there was an explosion, and she was on the ground," Jerry repeated.

"And?"

"I know Detroit has a reputation for being rough, but we don't get many explosions here in Port Hope," Jerry said dryly. "If there are guns involved, it's because of what I do, which means I am responsible for putting her in danger."

"I guess it could have been a premonition," Granny agreed.

Jerry intertwined his fingers and stared at the woman open-mouthed. "Is that supposed to make me feel better?"

"No, I don't suppose it should. It wouldn't make me feel better if I were in your place. Oh, don't mind me; I'm just an old woman thinking out loud."

Jerry took a deep breath and blocked her from his next thought. *No, you're not an old woman. You're dead.* Jerry unblocked her once more and looked at Gunter, whose head tilt showed the dog to be intently listening to their conversation.

Granny lifted the cup and took a sip before speaking. "Do you feel April is in danger?"

Jerry sighed. "I'm not sure."

"What does your gut tell you, Jerry?" Granny asked, rephrasing the question.

"That I am in danger of losing her," Jerry said, voicing his growing concern.

Granny raised an eyebrow. "You think this is because you didn't ask her to marry you?"

Jerry took a sip of coffee before answering. "She seems pretty hurt because I didn't."

"Hurt is reasonable; thinking she'll leave you because you didn't ask her to marry you isn't. Do you really think April is that shallow?" Granny asked.

Jerry smiled and looked at the ceiling once more. "April is the least shallow person I know."

Granny matched his smile. "She's also not about to let you push her away without a fight. Don't you think she deserves someone who'll fight just as hard to protect her?"

"I'd give my last breath to protect her and Max," Jerry said sincerely.

"Protecting them means letting them in, not coming up with reasons to push them away. To be honest, I thought you were done with that nonsense," Granny mused.

"Yeah, so did I." Jerry ran his hand over his head. "It's the dream…too many memories, and then when I saw April lying there…"

"Jerry, you have a future right here, and April needs you to be on your A game right now," Granny replied.

The hairs on the back of his neck stood on end as Jerry held the woman's gaze. "You know something."

She didn't respond.

Jerry felt his frustration rise. "Tell me."

"You know there's no easy button," she reminded him.

"This is April we are talking about," Jerry said firmly.

"And Max," Granny replied.

Max hadn't been in the dream; if Granny was including her, the woman obviously knew more than she was letting on. He pounded a fist on the table. "Tell me what you know."

Gunter sprang to his feet, growling at no one in particular. Jerry stared at the dog, wondering where his loyalty lay. A second later, Houdini appeared at Gunter's side, ears forward, tail erect, matching his father's stance.

Granny laughed a haunting laugh. "What was that you were saying about not being able to protect your family? Things have changed, Jerry. You have changed as well. You need to remember that you're not alone anymore. You've got the dogs now. Plus, you can't say boo without that boss of yours calling to see what's up."

"Fred? What does he have to do with all of this?"

"Lighten up, Jerry. It was a joke," Granny said when Jerry failed to laugh.

The dogs eased their stance and looked from Jerry to Granny as if trying to assess the situation.

Jerry called the dogs off. When he spoke, his frustration was evident. "Why won't you tell me what you know?"

"You know that's not how it works." A sadness touched her eyes. "You know I'm not allowed to give you information that will change the course of things."

"What things? I don't care about the rules. All I want to do is keep my family safe."

"And you will. It's what you do." She reached across the table and placed her hand on his. "I know it doesn't feel like it at the moment, but you have me too. I may not be able to give you all the answers you currently seek, but I'll be there, if and when you need me. The same goes for others you've met along the way."

"What others?"

Instead of answering, Granny slowly faded from view. As she disappeared, her words floated through the air. "You have friends on both sides. Use your resources, and if you find yourself in a pickle, don't be afraid to ask for help."

Chapter Two

Jerry pulled on his boots, opened the back door, and felt the bite of the wind blowing off Lake Huron. He shivered. While the calendar proclaimed it to be spring, the weather in Port Hope, Michigan, had yet to warm. He pulled on his parka and gloves as Gunter and Houdini raced past, running through the snow with abandon. Houdini stilled and surveyed the white pasture before dipping his head to taste the icy fluff. Spurred on, he raced through the yard, emitting eager yips as if he found this late spring snow to be the best present ever.

"Quiet, boy. People are trying to sleep," Jerry said, shushing him.

Mindless of the reprimand, Houdini ran through the yard, biting at the snow and chasing after Gunter, who also seemed pleased to be outside at this early hour. Caught up in their antics, Jerry reached into the snow, grabbed a handful, and rolled it into a ball. Seeing him, Houdini planted his feet, watching Jerry's every move. Jerry threw the snowball. Houdini raced after it, sticking his nose in the pile of snow where it landed. He pulled his nose free, looked at Jerry to see if he'd actually thrown it, and then buried his nose once more. Jerry glanced at Gunter. The dog cocked his head, looking at Jerry as if to say, *That boy has a lot to learn.*

Jerry chuckled, then picked his way to the fence, stomping along the barrier to mash down the snow to give Houdini an area to run without being belly-deep in the white fluff. Jerry knew his effort was in vain, as Houdini was now frantically digging into the snow, looking for the lost ball.

Jerry glanced at Gunter once more. "Are you going to tell him, or should I?"

Gunter smiled a K-9 grin that said, *Leave him be, he'll figure it out on his own soon enough.*

Making his way back to the house, Jerry debated going inside but opted to push the snow from the Adirondack chair instead. He sat and pulled his hood up to block the wind, then willed his mind to let him see into April's future, growing more impatient with each passing moment. It was his own fault; he knew better than to try to force the gift, but this was April, and so far, the only information he'd been given was the snippet from the dream. *Maybe I should go back to bed and see if I'm given anything else.* Too late, the dogs alerted, peering at the house, sniffing the air, letting him know either Max or April was awake.

Houdini took a step forward, looked at Jerry, and whined eagerly. This was great progress, as the pup often acted first and then used his soft brown eyes and wiggly behind to beg his forgiveness after the fact.

Jerry signaled the pup's release, then sighed as both Houdini and Gunter ran to the house, each disappearing without the aid of the doggy door. He scanned the neighboring windows to see if anyone had witnessed the feat, relaxing only when he didn't see or feel anyone looking. He wasn't worried about Gunter, as his ghostly partner was virtually invisible to most, but Houdini was an anomaly. Sired by Gunter, the pup was very much alive and could disappear at will unless wearing the specially-made harness constructed out of a rope given to Jerry by Clive Tisdale, the spirit of a Texas Ranger. While they didn't keep it on Houdini all the time, it did come in handy during times when they needed the dog to be less conspicuous.

Jerry started to follow the dogs inside but decided against it, knowing it was possible whoever had alerted them was merely going to the bathroom and would be heading back to bed when finished. If that was the case, he didn't want to keep them from doing so. Plus, he knew if either April or Max were truly up for the day, they would seek him out before long, if only to tell him to come inside before he froze to death.

He sat back in the chair and closed his eyes to settle his unease. Opening them once more, he scanned the windows of the nearby homes, still expecting to see someone peering out at him. While he loved that the house was nestled within the Village of Port Hope, the close proximity to the neighboring houses caused him constant angst when it came to the dogs. If any of the neighbors caught a glimpse of Houdini walking through walls, the sleepy little town wouldn't be the same. Even if he could get the neighbors to promise to keep their secret, most people were ingrained with the need to tell at least one person, who would then tell another until, before long, the area would be crawling with curious souls hoping to either catch sight of the ghostly canine or prove him to be a hoax.

Jerry closed his eyes once more and silently thanked the designer for finally forming house plans. The construction crew had already cleared the property and were on track to begin construction on the house outside of town in the coming days. At least out there, the only eyes he'd have to worry about would be April's friend Carrie, and she already knew about Houdini's special lineage.

Jerry placed his hand on his neck to soothe the tingle, then brought his hands together in prayer form before wrapping his fingers around the back of his hands and pressing his thumbs to his mouth. *What is it that has you so unsettled, McNeal?* The question was met with silence.

Not getting anywhere, Jerry pushed off the chair and started toward the house. On a whim, he decided to check the side gate before heading inside. He trudged through the snow and tugged on the gate, feeling somewhat relieved to find it latched in place. *Easy, McNeal, don't let yourself get paranoid.* Even as the thought came to him, his feeling told him he had a right to be worried. He walked to the house, contemplating his next move. His dream had warned of April being in danger, but Granny had mentioned Max. That had to mean something. As he stepped inside the house, he recalled his grandmother's words: use your resources and don't be afraid to ask for help. He pulled off his boots and coat and looked to the ceiling. "Help."

Gunter appeared at his side, wagging his tail.

Jerry's anxiety dwindled. He looked to the ceiling once more. "Message received."

Gunter tilted his head and gave him a look that said, *Does that mean I can go now?*

Jerry nodded, and Gunter disappeared. Calmer now, Jerry pulled his phone from his pocket and scrolled to find Fred's number. He typed out a message: > *Call me. Not urgent.* The cell rang even before the phone went dark. Jerry answered. "You're up early."

"Actually, I was sleeping until a second ago," Fred informed him.

"I distinctly recall typing 'not urgent,'" Jerry replied.

"McNeal, when have you ever sent me anything that didn't eventually lead to something significant?"

The man had a point.

"What's got you troubled at this early hour?" Fred asked.

"I don't know."

"I would get all irate about you waking me and tell you to call me when you have something, but I know better. So, tell me what you do know."

"I think April and Max are in danger, but it's early yet," Jerry said and went on to tell Fred about his dream."

"Your dream didn't involve Max?"

"No, I pinged on April, and Granny mentioned Max."

"How is it your dead grandmother can tell you Max might be in danger but doesn't tell you what the trouble is?"

"It's complicated," Jerry replied.

Fred chuckled. "McNeal, your whole life is complicated."

Jerry sighed. "Tell me something I don't already know."

"You want me to get a team up there?" Fred asked.

"No. Not until I know what we are dealing with," Jerry replied.

"What if it's too late by then?"

The man had a point. Jerry ran his hand over his head. While he wanted to keep his family safe, Port Hope was a small town; even if the men came incognito, someone would see, and before long, everyone would know. "Not here."

"Okay, where? I can send the jet and take you someplace safe."

Jerry rolled his neck. While keeping April and Max safe was the point, how long would be long enough to stay away? He thought of Susie and how she'd balked at living life under constant guard. "It wouldn't work."

"Why not?"

"I don't even know if the threat is real. Besides, you remember what happened with Susie. Eventually, they would demand to come home."

"What if Susie's the answer?"

Jerry frowned into the phone. "I'm not following you."

"You won't let me send in a team, so what about a team of one?" Fred replied. "Susie is the perfect choice. She is someone the girls know and trust and who won't raise suspicion. Heck, we don't even need to let them know. I'll have Susie call to say she needs a break and wants to come for a visit."

"Listen, I like Susie and all, but she's been through enough. If there's trouble, she'd only be one more person in harm's way."

Fred chuckled. "I guess the two of you haven't talked."

Jerry felt a chill race the length of his spine. "Talked about what?"

"Susie's part of the team."

"What team?"

"Your team."

Jerry's jaw twitched as he pulled out his wallet, snapped a photo of one of the business cards Fred gave him, and sent it to the man. That Fred hadn't questioned his silence let Jerry know his boss was giving him time to process the comment. "What exactly does Lead Paranormal Investigator mean to you?" Jerry asked when seeing the picture had been viewed.

"It means you are my go-to guy," Fred said coolly.

"I would think Lead means I am in charge. How can I be in charge of this so-called team if I don't even know who's on it?"

"Now, don't go puffing up on me. You don't seem to be much of a team player, so we didn't think to bore you with all the details."

Fred had a point. Jerry preferred to work alone. "Why call it a team in the first place?"

"What can I say? The accounting office demands a paper trail," Fred replied.

"The last I heard, Susie had a deep desire to own her own mortuary and had a well-thought-out plan of how and when she was going to get there."

"Sure, she had a plan, and she would have gotten there eventually. But with our help, she'll get there a lot sooner than she expected."

"If she is still going to be a mortician, what exactly is Susie's job with the agency?" Jerry asked, circling back to the point.

"In this case, she'll serve as a bodyguard to Max. She can shadow April if you need her, but mostly, she'll keep eyes on Max, since I'm assuming you'll be keeping close tabs on April."

Jerry had to admit he liked the idea of someone shadowing Max.

"Before you say no, I can assure you Susie can handle herself. She was good before, but she's spent the last year working with the agency to hone her skills."

"Why Susie?" Jerry knew the answer but wanted to hear the man say it.

"Because Max trusts her."

"That's not what I'm asking, and you know it."

There was a slight pause. "Because she has the gift."

"Her gift is not that refined," Jerry told him.

"She's working on that too."

I don't like it. "You're getting quite a collection," Jerry said, keeping his previous thought to himself.

"I prefer to think that I am gathering the perfect team," Fred retorted. "I'm looking out for you, McNeal, which includes using all the resources I have available to keep you and your family safe. You have a job to do that often takes you away from your family. Max is one of us now, and there will come a time when you'll both be working on a different case. When I saw how well Max and Susie got along, my first thought was to bring her into the fold in case we ever need her to watch over Max. I would think that foresight would warrant a bit of gratitude."

"I do appreciate you looking out for Max," Jerry told him.

"But?"

"But my gut tells me there is more to it."

"Is that the psychic talking or the person who has seen the movie *Firestarter* one too many times?" Fred asked.

I wish I knew, Jerry thought without committing.

"McNeal, if you have something to say, just say it. My days are already filled listening to a conspiracy theorist."

An image of Fred's partner Barney came to mind. "What does Barney have to say about this?"

"About this, nothing. Since our government has decided to admit to there being aliens, he's too busy dealing with the fallout."

Jerry eyed the phone. "I thought that was all smoke and mirrors. You're saying there are really aliens?"

His comment was met with a hearty laugh. "Mr. McNeal, how are you able to believe in ghosts but question the existence of aliens?"

"One I've seen. The other I'm expected to take on good faith," Jerry told him.

"Welcome to my world, McNeal," Fred said dryly. "I've yet to see a ghost, but here I am paying you and the others a small fortune to keep them from disturbing the status quo."

"You're forgetting that you saw Gunter on film playing with an elephant," Jerry reminded him.

"What was that you were saying about smoke and mirrors, McNeal? When I see the dog in person, then maybe I'll be in more of a sharing mood."

"Why, Mr. Jefferies," Jerry said, mocking the man, "are you implying you doubt the existence of my partner?"

"I'm saying in our line of work, sometimes good faith is all we have. I go to bed every night feeling a little safer knowing you are on my team. Listen, I hear the coffee pot calling my name. Susie Richardson is an asset and is very good at what she does. I can't force you to use her, but if it meant protecting my family, I'd use every tool at my disposal. Think about it and let me know."

"Let me see what Max has to say about this. Even

if we didn't tell her about Susie, she'd know," Jerry replied. "And, Fred."

"Yeah, McNeal?"

"Thanks."

"No problem. If you need anything else, say the word." The phone blinked, showing Fred had ended the call.

A shiver ran through Jerry as the wind shifted and brought with it a heavy snow squall.

Chapter Three

Giggles filled the air as April and Max entered the room, with Gunter and Houdini leading the way. Their giggles stopped the moment they saw him. Jerry blocked Max from reading him as he stood and embraced April.

April rewarded him with a kiss, then rubbed at the frown line between his eyebrows. "You were up early. Is everything okay?"

Jerry kissed her on the nose and released his hold. "Couldn't sleep." He turned and walked to the counter, poured her a cup of coffee, and handed it to her. "Your snoring kept me awake."

"I do not snore," she said, arching a brow.

"Oh, but you do. Only your snores are soft and comforting," Jerry said and winked.

Gunter groaned.

"I agree!" Max laughed.

April turned toward her. "You think I snore?"

Max shook her head. "No. Gunter said you two need to get a room and I told him I agreed."

April stiffened. "You're telling me the dog is talking to you?" She turned to Jerry. "Does Gunter really talk?"

Jerry laughed. "Gunter groaned. Max filled in the blanks."

April slapped a hand to her chest. "Oh, thank God."

Jerry eyed Gunter. "You don't think it would be cool if the dog could talk?"

"Not if the dog in question shares a room with us," April said, giving him a pointed look.

Jerry knew April was referring to their nightly escapades. He smiled. "Point taken."

"I heard you on the phone. It's early, so I'm assuming you were talking to Fred. Does that mean you'll be leaving soon?" April took a drink of coffee and looked at him over the cup.

"Yes, it was Fred. No, I'm not leaving."

"Oh," she replied, then covered her response by taking another drink.

Jerry looked from April to Max. "Why do I get the feeling you two were hoping I'd gotten an assignment?"

April blew out a sigh. "We don't want you to go anywhere. It's just that Max and I are planning on going to Frankenmuth for Osterbrunnen."

"It's the Easter Celebration. Mom and I go every year," Max said, jumping in. "We've been going ever since I can remember."

Jerry wasn't sure if he was getting a hit on his radar because this was the first time he'd heard of this, because they'd not extended him an invite, or because if he weren't there, he would not be able to protect them. Whatever the reason, the hairs on the back of his neck now tingled. "So, this pilgrimage is a mother-daughter thing?"

April glanced at Max before answering. "It can be if you want it to."

Jerry tried to get a read on Max and realized the girl had blocked him. He pushed off of the counter and sat at the kitchen table. Leaning back in his chair, he looked at April and Max in turn, then palmed his hands to the chairs on either side of him and waited for them to be seated. "Now, would one of you care to tell me what is going on?"

"Max was three the first time I took her to Frankenmuth," April said. "We were living with my parents, and I just needed to get away, even for a few hours. I had a full tank of gas, so I put Max in the car and just started driving with no real destination in mind. Then I saw a billboard for Frankenmuth. I hadn't been there in years, so I thought, *What the heck?* When we got there, the town was decorated with beautiful flowers and eggs for the Bavarian

Easter Festival. Max was only three, and seeing the way her eyes lit up as we walked through town was just magical. I realized she'd needed that trip just as much as I did. I didn't really think about it at the time, but now, knowing she is psychic, I just thought maybe all the negativity I was living with trickled down to her as well."

Jerry started to tell her the same thing would hold true even if Max hadn't been psychic, but he didn't want to interrupt her story.

"Anyway, I promised her that if we were able, we would go there for the festival each year."

"So, it is a mother-daughter thing," Jerry said, nodding his understanding.

April shook her head. "No. Randy went with us when I was married to him."

"Only because he was afraid we'd leave and never come back." Max's tone held venom.

"You and Max should go," Jerry said, even though he didn't like the thought of them going alone when something had his psychic radar tingling. "I've never been there myself. Maybe we can all go again when the weather warms."

"Or," April said softly, "you can come with us now, and we can all start a new tradition together."

Jerry glanced at Max, judging her reaction, and relaxed when the girl bobbed her head in agreement. He looked at April once more. "We have to learn to trust each other, Lady Bug."

Her brows lifted. "Of course I trust you."

"Not enough," Jerry replied. "I know it's early in our relationship, but someday, I hope you will realize I am not that guy. I love being with you and Max. I would gladly let you both go off and do your own things, but if I get a say, I'd prefer to do things together as a family." Jerry realized this was the perfect segue to proposing to them.

"Then why not tell us the truth?" Max said, pulling him out of the moment.

Jerry frowned. "What do you mean?"

"I got a bit of a reading just before you blocked me. You're worried about us, and you blocked me because you didn't want us to know."

"I blocked you because I'm not sure if there is anything to worry about and wanted to see if you came up with any hits on your own," Jerry corrected.

"Well, do you?" April asked, looking at Max.

Max closed her eyes for a moment. "No, I don't think so," she said, opening them once more.

April turned toward Jerry, relief evident in her voice. "I'm taking that as a positive sign unless you tell me otherwise."

"That Max hasn't picked up on anything is a very good sign," Jerry agreed. That his spidey senses hadn't pinged on anything since April and Max entered the room helped him sound more convincing than he actually felt. "It was probably just a bad dream."

"About us going to Frankenmuth?" April asked.

"No, I didn't know about Frankenmuth until just now. You don't have to keep secrets from me, you know?"

April sighed. "I'm sorry. I wasn't trying to keep it from you...I just didn't want you to feel pressured into going. Randy hated walking around the shops."

"I'm not Randy," Jerry said a little too firmly. He eased his tone. "Not only am I not trying to control you, but I love to shop."

April giggled and then caught herself.

"Care to tell me what is so funny?" Jerry asked.

"You shop like a girl," April said, and the giggle turned into uncontrolled laughter. "It's a good thing we're building a bigger house."

She was speaking of the fact that he could not go anywhere without bringing them back something that had caught his eye. "Would you prefer me not to bring you presents?"

"NO!" both April and Max answered at once.

"We love your gifts," April said sincerely. "I'm just saying I've never been around a man who enjoys shopping as much as you."

"You can thank Granny for that. That woman was always dragging me into one store or another. Only she didn't have a lot of money to spend. I'm telling you, that woman could surely hunt out a bargain." Jerry waggled his eyebrows. "Just wait until you see me in a thrift shop or antique store."

April smiled a genuine smile. "You like antique stores?"

"I do."

This time, it was Max who groaned. "Oh, no. Not you too!"

Jerry gave a knowing nod. "Let me guess, your mom always drags you into antique stores, and while she is enjoying herself, you are wondering why everything in the store seems to be yelling at you?"

"YES!" Max replied.

April frowned. "Maxine Buchanan, I had no idea, or I would never have taken you with me. Why didn't you ever say anything?"

"It's like Jerry said," Max replied. "You always seem so happy when we go."

"All the same, I will not be taking you to any more antique stores," April said.

"Sure we will," Jerry said before Max could reply.

"You just said you know what she's going through," April reminded him.

"I know because it was the same thing I used to feel. Remember me telling you about surrounding yourself with the white light?"

Max nodded. "Yeah."

"Granny showed me how to protect myself from the energy of people and objects by using white light. There are some other things we can try too, but just because you are empathic doesn't mean you can't enjoy the things you like to do. It is the same with me; I don't always like being in crowds."

"Does protecting yourself make the fear go away?" Max asked.

"Not always," Jerry answered truthfully, "but it does help."

"Maybe you can show Max what to do when we go to Frankenmuth," April said softly.

Jerry tried to keep his excitement to a minimum. "Only if you really want me to go."

"Yes, we do," April said, answering for both of them.

"Are there antique stores there?" Jerry asked.

"There are, but I think there may be something even better this time."

Okay, that piqued his curiosity. "Like?"

"Like a huge antique auction. I've been looking at the items being listed all week and am dying to get my hands on a few things."

Okay, he didn't particularly like her choice of words, but he hadn't been to an auction since before he joined the Marines. He smiled at the memory.

April stood and walked to the counter to refill her cup. She held up the pot. "Want some more?"

Jerry held out his cup. "Sure."

"I could be wrong, but it looked like you just took a trip down memory lane," she said as she filled his cup.

"The last estate auction I went to was with

Granny—when she was still alive," he added for clarity. He waited for April to return to the table before continuing. "It was before I joined the Marines. The sale was in Sevierville; that's in Tennessee. The couple had been huge collectors of just about everything imaginable, and they'd been advertising the sale for weeks. So Granny and I drove down in her old pickup truck, and when we got to town, I asked her which way to go to the motel. She told me we were not staying in the motel because she had her eye on something and wanted to have the money in case she got into a bidding war. In the end, she got outbid anyway, and we ended up sleeping in the bed of the truck fighting mosquitoes for nothing." Jerry chuckled at the memory.

"Oh, that sucks."

"Yes and no. She didn't need to spend money she didn't have on something she really didn't need. We had a good laugh about it after the fact, and she used the experience to teach me not to get so caught up in things that I couldn't make a rational decision. Hey, this gives me an idea. Seltzer has been trying to guilt me into going to Pennsylvania for Manning's wedding, but I wasn't really interested in going."

At the mention of Manning's name, Gunter lifted his head intently, listening in on the conversation.

"It isn't like we were great friends or anything, but now that I have Gunter, I kinda think maybe I owe it to the guy to go. So, why don't we all go together and make a vacation of it? Pennsylvania is filled with small towns and tons of antique stores."

Max lit up like a candle. "Can we, Mom?"

April didn't appear as excited. "I don't know. Were our names even on the invitation?"

"They haven't been sent out yet, but you and Max are family, so I'm sure there won't be a problem with you both coming."

April pushed from the chair. She went to the sink and rinsed out her cup. Though she hadn't said anything, Jerry knew the thing that unsettled April most was going to a wedding that wasn't her own, and he vowed to rectify the fact that he hadn't officially asked her to marry him yet. He chided himself for the hundredth time for not asking her to marry him at Christmas as he'd planned.

"You're going to love Frankenmuth, Jerry. Wait until you see Bronner's. The whole store feels just like Christmas!"

Jerry thought Max was reading his mind, then recalled having blocked her from reading his thoughts. "Oh really, how so?"

"Because it's the world's largest Christmas store. Every time we go there, it feels like Christmas is all around us."

"That's probably because we get a special ornament and something new for our Christmas village." April rubbed her arms. "It wasn't always that way. In the early years, we couldn't even afford more than a sandwich to see us through to dinner."

"Speaking of dinner, can we take Jerry to Zehnders?" Max asked.

"That's the chicken restaurant, right?" Jerry shrugged. "A person can read a lot of billboards while driving."

"Of course."

"What's the matter?" Jerry asked, seeing the crease in April's brow.

"I was just thinking of all there is to see in Frankenmuth. By the time the estate auction is over, we won't have time to see and do everything. Maybe we should skip the sale this time."

"But you've been looking forward to it," Max reminded her.

"There will be other sales," April said.

"But, Momma, what about the…"

"It's okay, Maxine," April said, cutting her off. "Jerry made a valid point about not spending money on things we don't need."

"There's no reason we couldn't get a hotel room and spend a couple of days seeing the sights," Jerry suggested. Once again, Max's face lit up, letting him know he'd possibly managed to save the day.

"You've always wanted to spend the night at the Bavarian Inn and walk the streets after dark without worrying about the deer when we're driving home. Can we, Momma?"

April smiled. "Since it looks as if I'm

outnumbered, how could I possibly say no? Providing there are rooms to be had."

"The hotel has pools, water slides, laser tag, and putt-putt golf! Wait until I tell Chloe. She's going to be so jealous!" Max said, reaching for her phone.

Jerry frowned. "I hate to rain on your parade, kiddo, but it snowed overnight."

"It doesn't matter. Everything is inside," Max said, tapping at her phone. The phone buzzed a second later. "I was right; she is jealous. She said her mom is taking her and her brother to Zehnder's Splash Village this summer."

"Splash Village is bigger. Are you sure you don't want to go there instead?" April asked.

"Maybe next year. I like the idea of walking to town from our hotel. It's what we've always dreamed about doing. I'm going upstairs to call Chloe. If she thinks Frankenmuth is cool, wait until I tell her we're going to Pennsylvania!" Max said, running from the room.

"Are you alright with all of this?" Jerry asked when Max was out of earshot.

"I'm more than okay with it. You have so many wonderful stories about your childhood. I don't really have anything worth telling. Since we met you, our life has been one adventure after another, and because of that, Max will one day have some incredible stories to share with her family. I think Max might be disappointed once she sees how big

Zehnder's Splash Village is compared to the Bavarian Inn. Then again, she's right. We've always dreamed of staying at the Bavarian Inn and walking to the shops."

"Frankenmuth is not that far. There's no reason we can't go back in the summer."

April's eyes lit up. "Oh, maybe we can go back when they have the hot air balloons or the car cruise."

"If just thinking about going back makes your eyes light up like that, then we can most definitely go," Jerry said, pulling her into his arms.

Chapter Four

Jerry's cell phone rang, showing Fred's call. "If you want me to go to work, forget it," Jerry said, answering the call.

Laughter floated through the phone. "Remind me again why I'm paying you."

"Because I'm the best at what I do," Jerry said confidently. "What's up, boss?"

"Relax, McNeal, I don't have anything for you at the moment. I just wanted to see if you've had a chance to speak with Max and April."

"I did. Max hasn't pegged on anything, and I didn't want to mention my dream."

"What about Susie?" Fred asked.

"Not yet. Look, it isn't that I wouldn't welcome the extra set of eyes; it's just I don't want to be the boy who cried wolf."

"How about a little vacation just to play it safe? I could invent a job just to get you all out of there for a while," Fred offered.

"It's already in the works," Jerry told him. "April and Max always go to Frankenmuth, Michigan, this time of year. Normally, it's a day trip, but I suggested we all go and spend a couple of days."

"When are you leaving?"

"Friday. We plan on staying until Sunday afternoon."

"Good. I'll make the arrangements."

"What arrangements?"

"Why, for the hotel, of course."

"I'm not following you, boss. This isn't work-related."

Fred chuckled. "McNeal, wherever you go, it turns into work."

"You're not wrong," Jerry replied. Even still, Jerry had the feeling there was more to it than Fred was letting on.

"I know I'm not. Give me a bit to do what I do, and I'll send you the information."

"Just so you know, Max has her sights set on the Bavarian Inn. Apparently, it is within walking distance of town and all the shops."

"I'll see to it," Fred said and ended the call.

Jerry put the phone on the table and sat back in his chair, interlacing his fingers. While he should feel relieved that Max didn't pick up on anything, his radar was still pinging. Subtle as it might be, it was still there, and while he'd told Fred not to mount the cavalry, he had no doubt that was precisely what the man was doing at this very moment. Not only would Fred get them a room, but he would know the background of everyone sharing the same floor. Jerry didn't put it past the man to plant some of his people in the nearby rooms. Jerry had warned him off so he would not feel guilty if Operation Frankenmuth, as it was probably now labeled, went off without so much as a stubbed toe. Then again, if things did heat up, he would welcome having a team in place.

Feeling a bit more settled, he revisited their conversation, focusing on the part where Max mentioned the town was a Christmas town. Both April and Max loved the town and looked forward to their trip there each year. He recalled that April had once said anniversaries of proposals were to be not only remembered but celebrated as well. What better way to celebrate than continuing their yearly pilgrimage to the Christmas town? Not to mention that this would help him remember the date. Jerry smiled. He already had the ring and had been racking his brain on how to propose ever since he chickened out at Christmas. Now, April unknowingly provided the backdrop for a proposal she would never forget. Perhaps he could find a Santa suit and follow her around. Then, when she was least expecting it, he could drop to one knee and ask her. His smile turned into a grin as the plan took shape.

April came into the room pulling him from his thoughts. "Do you want to make the hotel reservations, or do you want me to do it?"

"I'll take care of it," Jerry said. He left out the part about talking to Fred as he didn't want to worry her.

"Which Durango do you want to take? Mine or yours?"

Technically, they were both his, but April inherited the silver SUV last year when Fred furnished Jerry with a souped-up jet-black James Bond version of the ride, complete with a hidden arsenal stored where the sunroof should be. It also had a direct line to the agency, an emergency SOS button, and enough survival gear to keep them alive if they encountered trouble while on the road. "We'll take mine." He winked disarmingly. "More bells and whistles."

April smiled. "Uh huh, you just like it because it's fast. Just remember, we have a teenager who will be getting her license in a few years watching everything you do. Max adores you, Jerry. You know she's taking notes."

"Don't you worry about Max. Uncle Fred is not going to let anything happen to his little protégée. I'm sure he already has her on the waiting list for the best driving school the agency has access to and will make sure she gets combat driving instruction as well. By the time she gets her license, she'll be skilled at high-speed chase, J-turns, L-turns, and U-turns. She'll learn braking techniques, skid control, and handling multiple vehicles if they try to force her off the road." Jerry had gotten so caught up in the thrill, he'd forgotten who he was talking to and decided to tone it down. "She'll also be taught to wear her seatbelt and do the speed limit while keeping her hands at ten and two."

April narrowed her eyes. "And just why would anyone want to force my daughter off the road?"

Jerry smiled a sheepish smile. "Have you been down the lakeshore lately? Those evasive maneuvers come in mighty handy when trying to avoid deer."

April sighed. "I guess I should be happy she has the agency looking out for her."

Jerry nodded. "Max is a special girl and has a lot of people, myself included, who will do everything in our power to keep her safe."

April placed her fingers on her temples. "I think I just had a premonition. I saw Fred standing in a control room, ordering someone to maneuver a satellite to watch Max on her first date. Can he actually do that, or am I being silly?"

Jerry tilted his head. "I'm pretty sure you're not far off the mark. It wouldn't surprise me if Fred Jefferies has one aimed at us right now." While April laughed off the comment, Jerry half-expected a call or text from his boss confirming his assessment.

April walked to the window and looked out. "Thank you, Jerry."

Jerry stepped up beside her. "For what?"

"Everything, I guess."

Jerry wasn't sure how to respond to that.

"Before we met you, I had nothing. I could barely afford to put food on our table, much less anything else a teenage girl would want or need. Now, we have financial security and a secret family to watch over us. As if that wasn't enough, we have you."

"I also had nothing. Now I have you and Max and I'd give everything else up if it meant keeping you both safe."

April stared at him, unblinking.

Don't be a fool, McNeal. This is the perfect moment to ask her to marry you. No, I want it to be special. Jerry was torn - all he wanted to do was take her in his arms, profess his love, and beg her to be his wife. But he wanted his proposal to be memorable and profound, a story that would be shared with their children and grandchildren. Children? As in more than just Max?

"Are you okay?" April asked.

Jerry was grateful she was not able to read his mind, as he wasn't okay. "Yes, I was just admiring the way the sunlight was dancing off your hair."

"Mom, where's my bathing suit?" Max's voice sang out from upstairs, breaking the mood.

"It's in with the summer clothes!" April yelled. She leaned in and gave him a soft peck on the lips, then ran her thumb across his cheek. "Mr. McNeal, I don't know what's going on in that head of yours, but it's going to be okay."

"I love you," he said, then pulled her into his arms, kissing her so that her lips knew they'd been touched.

"Mom!" Max called once more.

April pulled away and looked at the ceiling. "The kid is psychic; you'd think she could find a dang bathing suit. I'd better help her find it before she tears the closet apart."

Jerry pressed his lips to hers briefly, then released his hold on her. "Let me know if you need me to muster a search party."

"Will do," April said.

April had no sooner left the room when Jerry's cell phone chimed. He pulled it out and clicked on the message from Fred.

Fred> *The hotel is booked. You have two adjoining rooms for the weekend, with the option of staying longer if the need arises. Just say the word, and I'll make it happen.*

Jerry typed the word "thanks," started to hit send, and edited his reply. > *Thanks for looking out for us, boss.* Satisfied, he hit send.

Granny appeared next to him, wearing a pale blue dress with tiny flowers. Jerry recognized the dress. People often worried about what they were to be buried in, thinking the choice would follow them to the great beyond. While he didn't know what went on behind the scenes, Granny often appeared in clothes he'd seen her wearing while alive. He preferred it that way, as it made her seem more alive. "You look nice."

She grinned and smoothed the dress with her hands. "Maybe you should ask him for a Santa suit."

That she had known his intention didn't come as a surprise. "I thought about it then figured he would make a big deal about it. Knowing Fred, he'd skip the suit and go straight to the source and ask him to propose. Besides, Christmas is over, and Santa has earned himself a vacation. I think this is more of a job for Santa's helper. I know I'm having a bit of a time finding the right moment, but I'll get there. And I could be wrong, but I think she would appreciate it more if I'm the one asking."

Granny giggled. "You think your boss really knows how to contact Santa?"

"If the man's real, I'm sure he could find him."

"Jerry Carter McNeal, don't tell me you've stopped believing in Santa Claus."

"Nope." Jerry winked. "A wise woman once told me that if I stopped believing in Santa, the magic of Christmas would disappear. I guess I'm not ready for that to happen just yet."

"Good. I hope you never stop believing." Granny moved across the room and sat at the table. Jerry took that as an invitation to join her.

"Something on your mind?" he asked, settling into his chair.

"I heard what you were thinking earlier… about maybe wanting more kids. I don't recall ever hearing that from you. Max is thirteen. Are you sure April wants more children?"

"We haven't discussed it if that's what you're asking."

"Do you think maybe you should, you know, before either of you finds yourself in a position to get your hearts broken?"

"We are well past that, but it's nothing for you to worry about. While I think it might be cool to have a little Jerry running around, I know nothing about raising children, and with my job keeping me away at times, I know April will be the one bearing the brunt of the child-rearing. She's already been through that with Max, so I'll not saddle her with that again. I love Max as if she were my own daughter, and if she is the only child in my life, I am okay with that. It will be April who makes the decision as to if there will be any more and I'll be fine with whatever she decides."

"You turned out to be such a good man, Jerry," Granny said, patting his hand.

"That's because I was raised by a good woman," Jerry replied.

"That's true, but don't discount the fact that you also had two parents who loved you even through your differences. Just because you weren't always with them didn't mean they weren't there for you. Don't let mistakes of the past keep them from knowing their grandchild or children, whatever the case ends up being. They have some good years left in them. You make sure they get a chance to meet your family. I know they will love Max as much as if she were of your blood."

"I'll make sure they get to know my family," Jerry promised.

"Good, because from what that child tells me, April's family has no business around them. I'm telling you, it is a wonder that child has turned out as good as she has with what she's been through, between April's parents and that no good ex-husband of hers."

The words had no sooner left her mouth than the skin on the back of Jerry's neck began to tingle. He leaned forward, crossing his arms and putting his elbows on the table. "Are you trying to tell me something?"

Granny's energy winked several times then disappeared completely.

Not wishing to be overheard, Jerry pulled on his boots, coat, and gloves, and stepped outside. The instant he shut the door, both dogs appeared in the yard with him. While Gunter kept a watchful eye on him, Houdini seemed content to revisit his earlier antics and ran through the yard with puppyish exuberance. Jerry dialed Fred's number.

Fred answered immediately. "McNeal?"

"What's the status with Randy?" Jerry asked as he walked along the fence line.

"Randy?"

"April's ex. Do you still have eyes on him?"

"I have a man on him," Fred replied.

Jerry wasn't satisfied. "Make sure. What do you know about the rest of her family?"

"Just what we've discussed previously. The family is dysfunctional, but none of them are serial killers. I believe there might be a traffic ticket or two, but no criminal records. Why do you ask?"

"Something Granny said," Jerry answered without going into further detail.

"Did the woman like you much?" Fred asked.

"Of course. She was my grandmother. Why?"

"I was just trying to see if there was a reason for the discombobulation. Seriously, why make you jump through hoops to get your answers?"

"According to her, there are rules, and she isn't supposed to say or do anything to change the course of things," Jerry replied.

"Be that as it may, I'm going on the record to say that if I die before you, I'm going to come back and tell you everything there is to tell."

Jerry smiled, knowing the man was as good as his word. "Roger that, sir."

"Good. Now that we've clarified that, do you need me to do anything besides check on our boy?"

"Yeah, send me an updated picture of the man." The request was probably unnecessary as his psychic radar would most likely ping if the guy were anywhere near, but if there were a lot of people milling about, it would be nice to know who he was searching for.

"You still planning on going away this weekend?"

"Yes. I don't think I could talk them out of it if I tried. Besides, I figured you already have the town wired."

"Why, Mr. McNeal, do you think I would go against your wishes?"

"In a heartbeat." Jerry chuckled.

"Have an uneventful weekend, McNeal."

"That's the plan, boss." Jerry pocketed his phone when he saw Fred had ended the call.

Chapter Five

April stood in front of the mirror, willing herself calm before heading downstairs. That Jerry and Max hadn't picked up on her unease meant she'd done a good job at blocking them. *You've got this, girl*, she told herself, then picked up her bag and carried it downstairs.

Jerry's gaze moved to the two previous bags she'd carried down on her own while he was in town, filling up the Durango with gas.

She sat the small bag next to the others. "I think this will do it. What's the matter?" she asked when his eyes took in the new bag.

Jerry shook his head. "Nothing."

"That's not a 'nothing' look," she said.

"You know we'll only be gone a couple of days, right?"

She looked at his single bag sitting next to him and laughed. "You may shop like a girl, but you pack like a guy."

"What's that supposed to mean?"

"It means you probably have two of everything: two pairs of pants, two shirts, two pairs of socks, two underwear, and maybe a pair of swim trunks."

He smiled. "Sounds about right."

"I have to prepare for all contingencies."

Jerry rocked back on his heels. "Like?"

"Like, I have an outfit for what the weather is supposed to be and two more in case it is warmer or cooler than what the weatherman says. Of course, some outfits require different shoes."

"Of course," Jerry agreed.

April suddenly had misgivings about bringing so much. "I can go through them again if you want," she said.

"No, we won't be needing the third-row seat, so there'll be plenty of room for this and anything we want to bring home as long as we don't go too crazy at the auction."

April glanced at the bags once more. "I forgot about the auction. Maybe I should combine the bags."

"Don't worry about it. If we find something big, either I can go back and get it, or we can rent a trailer."

Max came into the room and placed a backpack

next to the suitcases. "I'm all packed."

April sighed and blew at a strand of hair that had fallen in front of her face. "Where did I go wrong as a mother?"

Max wrinkled her brow. "Huh?"

"She's teasing," Jerry told Max, then looked in her direction. "Are you going to take Houdini to Carrie's?"

April nodded and waited for Max to spool up. She didn't have to wait long.

"Wait, you mean Houdini's not going with us?"

"Not this trip," April replied. "The hotel doesn't allow dogs and he's not certified yet."

"He can't stay here by himself." Max's voice was edged with panic as she turned to Jerry. "Can't Uncle Fred do something?"

"Not yet," Jerry said, backing April. "Fred's trainer will be back to test you both in two weeks. You're lucky the agency took an interest in his training and found a trainer to come up here and work with you both to get Houdini ready for service."

Max frowned. "He's already doing everything I ask of him."

"Yes, but he's still young, and some might question that. When he is fully certified, he will be a working dog. His job will be to protect you and track."

"He already does both," Max argued.

"Yes, but there are laws involved. If the agency is going to take responsibility for his actions, they need to make sure he is ready," Jerry told her.

"It's not fair." Max huffed. "Gunter gets to go."

April decided to step in. "Stop arguing with Jerry. You know Gunter is different."

"Houdini is different too."

"Which is why he excelled at his training," Jerry agreed.

"That's enough, young lady, or I'll leave you here with him. He's going to stay with Carrie," she added before her daughter decided staying home alone was a good idea. April smiled. "Don't worry, he will be fine. It's only for a couple of days, and you know Houdini adores Carrie."

Max brightened. "Can I go with you to drop him off?"

April shook her head. "No. I think it will be easier on both of you if you say your goodbyes here. If you go, he'll feel your anxiety and won't want to stay. This way, he'll be happy to go on a car ride. Take him outside and throw the ball with him for a few moments. It will help settle both of you."

"Okay," Max said, heading for the door. She started to call for Houdini when the pup darted past her and pushed his way through the doggy door.

"Good job telling her what she needed to hear," Jerry said as soon as Max was out of earshot.

April knew he was referring to their previous

conversation, in which she voiced the same concerns as her daughter. "I hope I sounded convincing. You know I'm worried something will go wrong."

Jerry arched a brow. "Still?"

"Yes."

"Huh, I'm surprised she didn't pick up on that."

"She can't." April smiled a cheesy smile. "I blocked her."

Jerry beamed his approval. "You're getting pretty good at that."

"I'm just glad I know how. That kind of thing comes in handy with a teenage psychic in the house."

"Back to Houdini, he will be fine. Just make sure to remind Carrie to keep the harness on."

"What if we need him?" April asked, speaking to the fact that the dog was his father's son and had a knack for appearing out of nowhere and helping control a situation when needed.

Jerry took a moment to consider this. "Tell her she will know if he's needed."

April looked out the window. "Ixnay on the trouble talk. They're coming back in."

Jerry answered with a quick salute. "Aye, aye, captain."

Houdini followed Max inside and waited for the girl to fit him with his harness. As soon as she clicked the clasp into place, Houdini began prancing around the kitchen, wagging his tail.

April called him to her. "Come on, boy, let's go for a ride." She gathered the leash from the hook on the door but didn't bother hooking it to the harness. They had great voice control over the dog, which didn't matter either, as nothing could pull his focus when he knew he was going for a ride. She smiled at Jerry and Max in turn. "I'll be back shortly."

"Drive safe," Jerry said and then looked over at Max. "We're going to see if we can fit your bags into the back of the Durango without a crowbar."

"Very funny," April said, heading to the door. Houdini beat her to the SUV and waited at the door. Getting the dog to wait for them to open the door before jumping inside had been one of the most difficult commands to train the pooch, who'd learned to just appear inside by mimicking his ghostly father. Jerry had finally had a long talk with Gunter, who now also waited for the door to be opened whenever the pup was around. April opened the door, and Houdini leaped into the backseat. While Gunter was permitted to ride in the front, Houdini knew his place was in the back, away from the front airbag. She climbed into the driver's seat and looked in the mirror. "Good boy."

Houdini woofed and answered with a K-9 grin.

It only took a few moments to drive to Carrie's house. As she turned into the driveway, Houdini whined as he paced the backseat. "You love your aunt Carrie, don't you, boy?"

Houdini answered with a string of eager barks.

Once parked, April opened the door to the Durango and waited for Houdini to jump down. The pup moved to her side as they walked to the house, then sat watching the door with eager anticipation. Carrie had on grey sweats with her brunette hair pulled back into a messy bun. She stepped aside to allow them in, giggling as Houdini greeted her with eager kisses.

April laughed. "He loves his aunt Carrie."

"My gosh, he's growing like a weed. He's huge. It's a good thing I made lots of doggie cookies." She stood and walked to the kitchen, Houdini on her heels.

April followed and watched as her friend pulled a treat from the jar. "Make him sit first."

Hearing the word "sit," Houdini sat even before Carrie finished giving the hand signal and command. "Good boy," Carrie said, handing him the homemade doggie biscuit. Brushing her hands together, she looked at April. "Any special instructions?"

"Nothing you don't already know. Just make sure to leave the harness on."

"You want him to sleep in it?"

"Keep it on the whole time so you don't have to worry about him disappearing."

"It's crazy that is even a thing," Carrie said, eyeing the dog. "Don't remove the harness, got it."

April nodded. "Unless he tells you to take it off."

Carrie lifted her eyes. "Did I miss something? I don't recall you saying the dog talks."

"No, but to be honest, I don't think it would surprise me if he did. I knew Jerry could see ghosts, then he told me Max could see ghosts, and enough had happened that I believed them, but I don't think I ever fully believed it until the day this guy disappeared. The first time it happened, Max and I were frantic. We looked everywhere for him until Jerry called to let us know Houdini was with him. The second time, we were more prepared and waited for Jerry's call."

"I don't know how you could be that patient," Carrie said, even though she'd heard the story before.

"We've learned that if Houdini disappears, there's usually a reason. Waiting for the call is easier than calling Jerry and not getting an answer. Then, my mind goes crazy with worry."

"You said he'll tell me…"

"You've seen how he acts if he wants to go outside and heard him bark if he hears something?"

"Yes."

"It's like that, but to the extreme, with whining and pacing and looking at you as if asking permission."

"What if he just misses you guys and wants to be with you?"

"That will be the usual moping with the occasional sigh. He does that when Max goes to school. I suspect he'll become your shadow and get even more clingy than he already is, so make sure you don't trip over him. I've been known to do that a time or two." April smiled. "Quit worrying. I promise you'll know the difference. Hey, I'd better get going before Jerry sends out a search party."

Carrie gave her a pointed look. "At least he would be doing it because he cares and not because he's psycho."

Everyone needs a friend who knows where the bodies are buried. For April, Carrie was that friend. Not only did the woman know all of her secrets, but she was also the only person who'd stood by her after Randy nearly killed her. Even before the man took it too far, he'd been abusive and controlling, rarely allowing her out of his sight. He'd told her on more than one occasion that if she ever turned on him, he would come back and finish what he'd started. If that weren't bad enough, he'd threatened to take Max from her. She hadn't heard from him since before the trial, during his incarceration, or since his release, but lately, he'd been invading her dreams. April rubbed her arms.

Carrie winced. "I'm sorry. I shouldn't have said anything."

"It's not that," April told her. "I had a dream about him last night, and it's got me a little wigged out."

"Another one? How many does that make?"

"Three in the last week." April rubbed her arms once more. "Max and I were walking around Frankenmuth, and Randy came out of nowhere, said he'd been looking for me and knew I'd be there this weekend because I'm always there. He didn't do anything in the dream, but I was scared because I knew he was there to do something." As if feeling her distress, Houdini came up beside her and sat on her foot, leaning into her.

"What did Jerry say?"

"I didn't tell him," April said, petting the dog.

"Huh, he's psychic. You're telling me he didn't pick up on it?"

"I blocked him and Max from reading me."

Carrie scowled. "April Buchanan, have you lost your mind? It could have been a premonition. Why on earth would you block them?"

April laughed, though there was nothing funny about this. "It was a stupid dream, not a premonition. I'm not the psychic one, remember?"

"What if…"

April cut her off. "It was only a dream. Listen, you know as well as anyone how hard I've worked to keep that jerk from taking up space in my mind. I've shared my past with Jerry, but I don't want him to think of me as a damsel in distress that he has to protect every moment. I want him to ask me to marry him someday, but I want him to do it because he wants to. Not because he feels some sense of duty to protect me."

"He's a man and a Marine at that. Protecting the ones they love is what they do. Well, most of them anyway. Every now and then there's a rotten apple in the bunch."

"Jerry does a good job of it," April told her. "You know I've had these dreams before, and nothing has ever come of them. I'm sure the only reason I'm having them now is because of what weekend it is. It is my own fault. They started when I changed the calendar to April. Then yesterday, I was packing and thinking of all the times Max and I have gone to Frankenmuth. One thing led to another, and I remembered the times Randy went with us. That's all there is to it. Can't you see, if I tell Jerry and Max about the dream, they'll be worried the whole time. I'm not going to give Randy that much power over us. I just want us to have a fun family weekend without any craziness. Even though I blocked him, Jerry is acting like he's walking on eggshells around me. He said he had a dream."

"Did you ask him what it was about?" Carrie asked.

April shook her head. "No, he didn't seem to want to talk about it. He asked Max if she felt anything, and she said no. So that proves everything is fine."

Carrie blew out a long sigh. "I guess you're right. But I still worry…"

"You always worry about me," April reminded her. "See, that is what I'm talking about. I've told you about the dream, and now you are going to worry about me until I get back here. Tell me I'm wrong."

"No, you're not wrong. Do you have a plan?"

"Plan?"

"If Randy shows up."

"Yep, I'm going to scream. If that doesn't bring in the cavalry, then I'm going to clock him." April giggled. "Max has me doing kickboxing videos."

Carrie lifted an eyebrow. "Since when?"

"A week now."

"You don't think she knows you're going to need it, do you?"

"No. She and Granny were watching videos on her phone, and the woman told her that they could come in handy in her line of work. Max agreed with her, and she's been practicing ever since. Sometimes, Granny and Bunny join us. Of course, I can't see either of them, but Max lets me know when they are there."

Carrie looked at her without blinking.

"What? I know I've told you about Bunny. She's the spirit with the pink hair. She isn't always around, but she shows up from time to time."

"It wasn't so long ago that if Max came to you

with stories like this, you'd have thought your daughter was losing it. Now you're standing here talking about her having conversations with spirits as if it is the most natural thing in the world."

A chill raced the length of her spine. "And I have you to thank for it. Let's be honest, we both knew where things were headed. If you hadn't seen the article about Jerry in the paper and encouraged me to reach out to him, I might be looking at having Max committed. Dang, girlfriend, maybe you're a guardian angel yourself. You helped me to get away from Randy and were instrumental in bringing Jerry into our lives. I don't know what I did to deserve you as a friend, but I owe you so much and don't have a clue how I'll ever be able to repay you," April said through a string of tears.

Carrie wrapped her arms around her. "We're friends. You don't owe me anything. Just promise to stay safe, and if you do find yourself tangling with Randy, clobber him once for me."

"I promise," the words came out in a sob.

"Good. Now stop crying before you make me start. Go to the bathroom and wipe your face so your Marine won't see you've been crying."

Carrie had always referred to Jerry as "her Marine" and she'd never once thought to correct her friend. Mainly because from nearly the moment she'd met him, she hoped it would become true. Even when he'd left Port Hope after coming to help

Max, something inside told her he'd be back. As that thought came to her, it was both comforting and a touch frightening. Perhaps she was a bit psychic after all.

Chapter Six

In the two days since deciding to go to Frankenmuth with April and Max, Jerry's feeling had yet to become more than a tingle. While his radar still pinged, it had not evolved into more than a slight tingle at the neckline. The fact that April was sitting next to him, and he didn't get a hit, allowed him to relax. While something was in the air, it was not centered around her as he'd originally thought.

The skies were a brilliant blue. The temps had warmed enough to melt what snow had been on the ground, and traffic on State Rte. 46 W. was, for the most part, nonexistent. With April and Max along for the ride, Jerry was enjoying the drive more than any he'd taken of late. Just an ordinary family of three on their way across Michigan's thumb for a weekend of fun.

Jerry glanced in the mirror and saw Granny and

Bunny flanking Max. All three had on headphones, staring straight ahead while Gunter looked out the back window as if wondering why they'd left Houdini behind.

Jerry concentrated on the road and reassessed his thoughts. *McNeal, there is absolutely nothing ordinary about your life.* It was true, yet at the moment, he was happier than he'd ever been – he hadn't worked the bugs out of things yet, but if all went as planned, April would be wearing an engagement ring on their return home. He reached across the console and breathed a sigh of contentment when she placed her hand in his. He started to rub his thumb on her finger where the engagement ring would be, then thought better of it, not wishing to give away the surprise.

"You look happy," April said.

"I am. Normally, when I leave Port Hope, I'm heading to points unknown all by my lonesome."

April laughed. "From the way you talk, you're never alone."

"Having company doesn't make me any less lonely for those I love," he said and gently squeezed her hand.

"I think I would get bored of all the driving," April replied. "Doesn't it bother you?"

"Not really. I guess I'm used to it. I drove all over the state of Pennsylvania when I was a trooper."

"I thought you just stayed near Chambersburg."

"I did toward the end. In the beginning, I went where they sent me, then Seltzer let me follow my feelings. That was a nice tour until the higher-ups stepped in and accused him of playing favorites. Maybe he was because he never asked any of the others where they wanted to patrol on any given day, but it wasn't like I was using my gifts for malice."

"Do you miss it?"

"Yes and no. I did love being a state trooper, but in the end, I didn't like it because it was the same as being in the Marines, where I knew something bad was going to happen, but I couldn't always do anything about it." He started to tell her that was his biggest fear about making a commitment to her and Max, but he didn't want to mar the trip with things he couldn't change. "I miss Seltzer and June and even Manning, even though the guy was a pain in my behind."

"There's your turn to Frankenmuth," April said, pointing. "Manning, that's the guy you said is getting married?"

Jerry flicked the blinker to go left and slowed to make the turn. The moment he turned onto Gera Road, he saw the sign indicating that it was six miles to Frankenmuth. "Yes, he was Gunter's handler before…" Jerry looked in the mirror, saw Gunter staring at him, and let the sentence drop.

"I'm glad Gunter is with us now. I mean, I know he's attached to you, but he helped Max in the bathroom when Ashley was haunting her, and went after that dog when Max and I were riding bikes. Not to mention how many times he's saved you. I know it sounds crazy, since I've never actually seen him, but I feel like he's here for a purpose, and part of that purpose is keeping my family safe. It gives me comfort when you're on the road and when Max is out of my sight. I just wish we didn't have to leave Houdini behind. I like how he protects Max and me, plus it helps that I can actually see him."

Jerry slid a glance in her direction. "You did tell Carrie what to watch for?"

"Of course."

Jerry nodded. "Then don't worry about him. If he is needed, he'll come."

"It's crazy."

Jerry smiled. "Yes, ma'am, it sure is."

"Were you serious about us all going to Pennsylvania?" April asked.

"Absolutely."

"Good. I'm looking forward to meeting Sergent Seltzer and his wife."

"Not as much as they're looking forward to meeting the two of you." Jerry saw the town come into view, along with the blue water tower off to the right with Frankenmuth written on it, and noticed there were more cars on the road than they'd seen during the nearly two-hour trip. He looked in the mirror, saw Max smiling, and grinned. "Wow, talk about a day trip. I'm used to driving all day, and we're already here."

"Almost. The heart of the town is just a couple blocks away," April said, pointing straight ahead.

April was not lying about it being the heart of the town. As they passed the grain mill, the architecture of the buildings took on the appearance of a quintessential German town with Franconian-style architecture with timbers placed in square and x patterns. The x's were carried through in many of the windows within the buildings. Even the hotels they passed along the way were molded to fit in. Traffic slowed, and Jerry let his gaze rove over the shops that lined both sides of the street. Frankenmuth Cheese Haus, Frank's Muth – which touted a full-service bar along with a popcorn bar and gifts. He looked to the right. "Oh, they have a Fudge Shop."

"Fudge, ice cream, pizza," Max said gleefully.

"And chicken," Jerry said. "I've seen those signs all up and down the interstate."

"Our hotel is over there! We need to go over the covered bridge!" Max shouted.

Jerry glanced in the mirror and saw she'd removed her headphones. She was frowning and looking to the left. He followed her gaze and felt a slight pull. "Don't worry, I'll turn around in a minute. First, I want to check out the rest of the town. Where'd everyone go?" he asked, seeing her sitting alone in the backseat.

"Where'd who go?" April asked.

"Granny and Bunny were riding with us. Now they are gone," Jerry replied.

"They left the moment you pointed out the fudge shop." Max laughed. "I'm surprised Gunter didn't go with them."

"I'm sure he'll find something to satisfy his sweet tooth before the day is over," Jerry said. He nodded to the horse-drawn carriages. "Have you guys taken a carriage ride yet?"

"No, but we've always wanted to," April said, looking out the window.

Jerry made a mental note to add a carriage ride to the to-do list and glanced at the cluster of intriguing shops on the left.

April pointed to the shops. "That's River Place Shops. They have a bunch of specialty shops and wine stores, which we will be able to walk to from our hotel. The walkable shops are pretty much concentrated in this part of town. The clock shop is there on the right, and now you've just about seen all the shops except for Bronner's and Zehnder's Splash Village. We can drive past them and turn around so you can see the welcome sign coming into town. The word 'welcome' is in German. Grandpa Tiny's Farm is near the sign; it opens in May. It's a centennial farm. They have pumpkins in the fall, and Santa and his reindeer come for a visit before Christmas, and then they close in the winter."

"There's Zehnder's Splash Village! Whoa! Look how big it is now!" Max shouted from the back seat.

"Max, lower your voice before you burst Jerry's eardrum."

"I'm sorry," Max countered.

Jerry drove through the parking lot without stopping. Taking in the massive glass-paneled structure on the northwest side of the hotel and the double waterslide tubes flanking the glass portion of the building, he could see why Max had gotten so excited. "If the inside looks half as good as the outside, I'm sure it's a lot of fun. Your mom and I are talking about coming back. Maybe we can stay here next time."

"Wow, you mean coming here twice in one year?" Max said.

"Sure, why not? It isn't that far of a drive."

"Until now, we've only come once a year, and spending the night was never in the budget," April explained.

"It's even better than the pictures Chloe had on her phone," Max said.

"That's because they just finished a huge renovation," April replied.

"Chloe is going to be so bummed she didn't get to see it before me."

April pointed to the next parking lot. "Keep going. Bronner's shares the parking lot."

Jerry continued through and passed a giant

snowman and a pile of painted ornaments, neither of which would fit in the back of the Durango. He wound his way to the expansive green and white building. "I figured it would be a decent size, but it's bigger than I expected." Jerry noted a clock near the west entrance that measured time in months instead of years. "Can you believe I saw a billboard for this place on I-75 in Florida?"

"That doesn't surprise me," April replied. "People come from all over to visit. Even walking through town, you'll hear tourists speaking many different languages. I remember reading that Bronner's is three hundred and twenty thousand square feet. The place is truly magical, especially when you walk in there for the first time. I know it sounds silly, but each time I go in there, I get butterflies. It's like they somehow managed to bottle Christmas spirit and have it sprayed into the air, infecting everyone who enters. If you stand inside the door and watch, you can see everyone's face light up like a child seeing the tree filled with presents for the first time on Christmas morning."

Jerry knew just the look of wonder April was speaking of, as it was on her face at this very moment. He pulled to the edge of the parking lot, pointed out several longhorn cows at the centennial farm, and took a left, driving under the sign that showed they were leaving Frankenmuth. "AUF WIEDERSEHEN, Frankenmuth," he said, wheeling the Durango around and heading back to town. As he neared the sign, he read the words from this direction. "WILLKOMMEN in Frankenmuth."

"You're going to be drinking beer and wearing lederhosen before the weekend is done," April told him.

Jerry laughed. "Beer, I can handle, but I don't see me wearing leather pants."

"That's probably a good thing," April agreed.

Jerry moved Bronner's to the top of the list of possible proposal sights. As he did, he noted the old black iron bridge and saw a man in a coat and hat waving at him. He blinked, and the man was gone. "That must have been the original bridge into town," Jerry said as they passed Bronner's once more. He passed the shops and smiled when he caught the green light toward the covered bridge. As he approached the bridge, he noted the brick road leading onto the bridge, whose signage stated the Holz Brucke (wooden bridge) was built in 1979 and had a seven-mile-an-hour speed limit. His smile evaporated when he saw a balding, thick-bellied man with a white beard standing in the middle of the bridge as if daring them to cross. The man wore red pants, with matching suspenders and a white shirt, and, for all appearances, looked like Santa Claus, without the famous red suit.

Jerry glanced at April, who stared straight ahead, oblivious to the not-so-jolly soul, then lifted his gaze to the mirror to see Max gaping at the man. Jerry stifled a chuckle. *Nope, nothing normal about my life at all.* He met Max's gaze and then gave a slight nod to April as he willed Max to hear him. *Have you ever seen him here before?*

Santa? Max asked, using her mind to answer.

He's not the real Santa, Jerry told her.

I know. But he looks like him. No, I've not seen him before.

We'll deal with him later if he's still here. For now, it's best if we don't let him know we can see him.

Though she didn't appear pleased, Max bobbed her head and sucked in her breath as Jerry drove straight through the man.

April turned in her seat and looked at Max. "Are you okay?"

"Yep, just excited to be here," Max lied.

"I love that you still enjoy coming to Frankenmuth." April shifted in her seat. Looking forward once more, she exhaled a sigh of her own. "I'm excited too. Maybe it's just because we're seeing it through Jerry's eyes, but it's almost as if we're seeing it for the first time," April said over her shoulder.

"Things definitely look different today." Max giggled. "I can almost feel Christmas running right through me at this very moment."

Jerry beamed. Max might not be of his blood, but at the moment, he was filled with fatherly pride.

Chapter Seven

Jerry stepped out into the hall and saw a man leaning against the wall at the end of the hallway, looking at his phone. Dressed in flamingo shorts, sneakers, and a Michigan T-shirt, the guy looked up when Jerry shut his hotel door, then turned his attention back to his phone. Normally, Jerry wouldn't think anything of it, but it was the same fellow he'd seen in the same place when they'd arrived four hours earlier and the one who'd shown up and hung out alone in the pool area the entire three hours they were downstairs. While the man hadn't joined them in the elevator, he'd disappeared from sight the moment April and Max grabbed their towels, and had resumed his place in the hall by the time they'd gotten off the elevator. That was thirty minutes ago, and the man was still in the same location.

Jerry figured he was probably one of Fred's boys; then again, Fred's team was normally a bit stealthier than this clown. Thankfully, neither April nor Max had noticed the man, but that was merely because they weren't trained to look for such things. He made a mental note to go over a few safety precautions to keep them safe in the future. He considered doing it now, but he didn't want to let on that his spidey senses were still on alert.

Gunter appeared at his side.

"Yo, dog, good timing. I was just about to go have a little chat with our friend over there."

Eager to get in on the action, Gunter trotted down the hall ahead of him and had already started his own sniffing investigation before Jerry reached the man. That Gunter hadn't donned his K-9 vest let Jerry know the dog didn't perceive the man as a threat.

The man swatted away the unseen nuisance and looked up when Jerry neared.

Not wishing to give the guy any unnecessary information, Jerry decided to cut to the chase. "Do you know who I am?"

The man shrugged. "Should I?"

"Let's put it this way, since my family is on this floor, and you are on this floor, and seem to have been watching us since our arrival, it would be better for you to know who I am than not. So, I'll ask you again. Do. You. Know. Who. I. Am?"

The man nodded.

Oh, for Pete's sake. Jerry nodded to Gunter, who moved in for a more personal sniff. The man's eyes grew wide, and Jerry smiled a knowing smile. "Tell me, or it will get worse."

"You're Jerry McNeal. My name is Carter; Fred Jefferies sent us."

Jerry relaxed, and Gunter moved away from the man. "Us? Just how many?"

"If you know Mr. Jefferies, then you must know he operates on a need-to-know basis." Carter gave a hapless shrug. "I'm pretty sure I'm not the only agent here in the building, or even on this floor. Unless the man in the room two doors down from you is trying to cool a body, ain't no one needs that much ice. Then there is the hot babe."

"Hot babe?"

Carter nodded. "Across the hall from the room next to yours. She arrived early this morning. I'm pretty sure she's one of us just by the way she carries herself. When this here is all over, I'd like to spend an hour or two in her room. I'm sure she'd be a welcome relief."

Fred had gotten them adjoining rooms, so the babe in question would be across the hall from Max's room. Instantly, he thought of Susie Richardson. "This woman, is she a redhead?"

The man grinned as if he'd just pulled a prize out

of a machine. "You know her?"

Jerry looked over his shoulder. "I've met her a time or two."

"Fantastic! Jerry, my man, you can introduce us!"

Jerry looked the man over. Not only was he a head shorter than Susie, but he was practically drooling over the possibilities. Jerry shook his head. "Nope. You're not her type."

"What's her type?"

"Stiffs."

"You mean she prefers a man in a suit? I can wear a suit."

"I mean, she's a mortician."

"You're saying she..."

"I'm saying the woman has had her share of tough knocks and doesn't need someone toying with her."

"It sounds like maybe you were hoping to keep that little tart all to yourself. Since you came with someone else, I guess I'll just let Red decide what she is or isn't ready for, unless you find yourself spending the night across the hall. Then I'll have to take my chances with that hot little number you came with."

Why, of all the arrogant...

Gunter growled.

Jerry stepped forward, blocking the dog's path, and placed his hand on the wall to the left of Carter's head. Reminding himself that Fred probably wouldn't want him to castrate the man, he leaned in inches from the man's face and evened his tone. "Mess with either of those women, and they'll never find your body. Capiche?"

The man's face remained stoic as he gave the slightest bob of the head.

"Good," Jerry said, pushing off the wall. "Now, how about you quit daydreaming and do the job you're here to do? My family gets in trouble because your mind wasn't on the job and…"

The man cut him off. "Just so we're clear, the only reason I'm going to let you walk away is because we're playing for the same team."

Only if that team is ogling women. Easy, McNeal, the guy was just talking out of his rear. Jerry worked to temper his response. "I'll be seeing you around, Carter."

"Don't worry, McNeal." Carter looked past him. "I promise not to let your family out of my sight."

That Carter had spent all afternoon staring at April in her bikini had Jerry more on edge than the feeling that had been swirling around for days. It took everything he had to turn and walk away without following through with his primitive instinct to punch the man. He debated about knocking on Susie's door, then decided against it. If she was here, she and Fred had already devised a cover story. He passed by his room and walked to the elevator. The door slid open. Jerry stepped inside and held the door as he addressed Gunter. "I'm just going to the lobby to call Fred. Keep an eye on the ladies for me, will you?"

Gunter yawned a squeaky yawn.

"It's okay. I promise to call for you if there's trouble," Jerry said and let go of the elevator door. He dialed Fred's number the moment he stepped off the elevator on the ground floor. The call went to voicemail. "Call me." Jerry ended the call and walked until he found a place where he could reasonably talk without being overheard and waited for Fred's call. He didn't have to wait long.

"McNeal, I thought we were going to keep this mission under wraps. It will be harder to keep your family under surveillance if you keep going around introducing yourself to my guys," Fred said the moment Jerry answered.

That Carter had run to his boss came as no surprise. "The man has no idea about being incognito. He wore flamingo swimming trunks and tennis shoes with socks to the pool. I had him pegged from the moment I saw him. Plus, if he doesn't keep his trap shut, I'm going to introduce him to my fist," Jerry said sourly.

"Carter said you seemed wound a bit tight. Perhaps you should go submerge yourself in the hot tub," Fred suggested.

"He was making lewd comments about Susie,"

Jerry told him.

"Such as?"

"Said he wanted to spend some time alone with her," Jerry said lamely.

"Have you seen Ms. Richardson lately?"

"No, I was going to knock on her door, but your man had already insinuated that I was upset because I wanted her for myself."

Fred chuckled. "I'm impressed by your self-restraint. Why, I would have put money that you would've reacted differently. Personally, I'm surprised you didn't clobber the man."

"Mentally, I did, but that was after he told me if I found myself too busy with Susie, he would settle for April."

"And the man's still alive?"

"Sorry to disappoint. I did threaten to kill him if he even looked at them sideways again. Does that make you feel any better?"

"It does. It also fills in the blanks of his side of the story." That was the thing about Fred. He was always eager to get to the bottom of things. "Do you want me to pull him?"

I want you to use him for target practice. Jerry kept that thought to himself. "No, he can stay, but you need to know, I'm not the only one who heard him disrespect the ladies."

"Meaning?"

"Meaning Gunter was there, and the dog takes

protecting those he loves personally."

"Did you tell him about the dog?"

"Nope." Jerry smiled. "I take it he hasn't heard it from you either."

"I like to keep my assets under wraps until needed," Fred reminded him. "So, what can Mr. Carter expect?"

"Why? So you can warn him?" Jerry asked.

"No, because I want to know how to tell it was the dog."

"Trust me," Jerry replied. "When Gunter makes his move, we'll all know."

Fred laughed. "Just make sure you're not in proximity when it happens. That kind of paperwork is such a mess to sweep under the rug. In all seriousness," Fred warned, "do try to stay clear of the man. In our line of work, enemies are well-trained with resources that expand normal reach."

"You're saying Mr. Flamingo poses a threat?" Jerry asked, picturing the man.

"I'm saying I have certain parameters when selecting my teams. Some are good for hunting things, and some are good for disposing of them. I'm not discounting your fortitude when it comes to protecting yourself or those you love, but I selected the man for this mission for a reason."

"Roger that, sir," Jerry replied. "So, what's the plan with Susie? I think it's safe to assume you have one."

"It is already in place. In about an hour, Ms. Richardson will reach out to Max to let her know she is in Saginaw for a conference and to say how she plans to drive to Port Hope to see you all if that is okay. Max will tell her you're in Frankenmuth, and she will just happen to find herself staying in the room across the hall."

"Not bad."

"Of course, it's not bad; it was my idea," Fred told him. "I'll debrief you both after this is over. I want to make sure my assessment of teaming Ms. Richardson and Max for future assignments is correct. If you see a problem, you say the word, and I'll look at putting something else in motion."

"There is one other thing."

"What's that?"

"Since April and Max are part of my life now, and April will be following Max on assignments, I want them both to have more training."

"What kind of training are we talking about?" Fred asked.

"It's just the usual stuff—situational awareness and such. Carter has been on my radar since I entered the building, and neither of them has given him a second glance. I can tell them, but they might think I'm just being overprotective and not take it as seriously as if it were to come as agency training."

"We'll get something set up," Fred promised.

"Oh, and I may have told April you would put

Max in a driving course when the time comes," Jerry admitted.

"Anything else?" Fred asked.

"Not yet, but give me time, and I'm sure I'll think of something." Jerry laughed.

"Go be with your family, McNeal, and do try to allow the team to do its job."

Jerry turned to see Bunny watching him. Sporting her usual pink hair, she was wearing a teal short-sleeved T-shirt that read "Frankenmuth, Michigan, EST 1904."

The pink-haired spirit frowned. "Why so glum, Jerry? You look like a kid who's just been scolded."

He placed his phone to his ear so he could talk without being labeled a kook. "I was."

"Tell me who to haunt, and I'll get to it!" Bunny said, narrowing her eyes.

For a moment, he thought of sending her to see Carter, then shrugged off the thought. The guy might be a pig, but other than flapping his jaw, he hadn't actually done anything to bring down the wrath of a spirit who didn't know if she was coming or going. Besides, he was pretty sure Gunter would take him to task before the weekend was over. "It's okay. I just had a couple of words with my boss, who told me to cool my jets."

"Oh, you must be moving up in the world if your boss gave you a jet," Bunny replied.

"He didn't give me a jet. He told me to cool them.

He wants me to behave," Jerry said when she furrowed her brow.

"Phooey on him," Bunny replied.

"I've got to get going," Jerry said, knowing the spirit would keep him there all day if not.

"Okay, Jerry. I've got to go find Betty Lou anyway. I really like your grandmother; once she loosens up, she's fun. Why, since we've been here, we've tasted the fudge and gone wading in the fountain. That's the thing about being on the other side; we can do anything we want, and no one cares." Bunny sighed. "Well, almost no one."

It was Jerry's turn to be concerned. "Problem?"

"There's a sourpuss downtown scaring all the tourists."

"Does this sourpuss look like Santa and hang out by the covered bridge?"

Bunny's brilliantly colored eyes bugged. "You've seen him?"

"Yes. He seemed upset."

"That's putting it mildly. Not only is he guarding the bridge, but he's also running around town messing with the tourists. He's even scaring the horses. Of course, the carriage drivers don't have a clue as to why their horses are acting up. They've tried to go out twice today and ended up having to turn back and refund the couple's money. He showed up while Betty Lou and I were in the Fudge Kitchen and nearly tripped the poor man carrying the copper kettle. He would have if me and Betty Lou wouldn't have…" Bunny giggled. "Okay, never mind what we did, but seriously, that can't be good for tourism – him running around like that and dressed like Kris Kringle, no less. Doesn't he know there are children who can see him? Maybe you should remind him of that. Yes, I'm sure you should. Tell him people are here to have a good time and can't, all because jolly ol' Grumpy Pants is being a pain in the behind."

"We are going downtown shortly. If I see him, I'll have a chat with him and try to figure out what's got him out of sorts."

"Okay, Jerry, but Betty Lou said to make sure you take Gunter with you." She looked around. "Where is he anyway?"

"Upstairs, keeping an eye on April and Max. Speaking of which, I'd better head back upstairs and see if they're ready. We're going to get something to eat and do a bit of shopping."

Bunny clapped her hands together, giggled a girlish giggle, and disappeared.

Nope, nothing normal about my life, Jerry thought, pocketing his phone.

Chapter Eight

Snow swirled through the evening sky, lending a Christmasy feel to the quaint Bavarian town. Then again, it could be because Jerry's hands were full of bags from purchases he, April, and Max had made. Jerry started to go into the fudge shop, saw the sign for the ice cream store and turned down the street.

"Where are we going?" Max asked.

"Ice cream!" Jerry replied, smiling when Gunter raced in front of him and pushed his way through the glass door.

"Jerry McNeal, we just left Zehnder's an hour ago. How on earth can you still be hungry after eating all that chicken?" April asked.

Jerry stopped at the door and winked at April while waiting for Max to open it. "I'll have you know there is always room for ice cream." The sweet fragrance of freshly baked waffle cones greeted them the moment they stepped inside the ice cream shop. Decorated in primary colors, the store reminded him of a preschool classroom, right down to the boldly checkered floor.

A young woman wearing a white shirt and blue apron dress with a ring of flowers weaved into her hair looked over the ice cream case and eyed his bags. "I'd ask what I could get for you, but I don't think you'll be able to carry it."

"I'll manage," Jerry said. It was warm in the shop, so he shifted his packages and unzipped his jacket.

"Or," April said, stepping up beside him, "you can stop being a Neanderthal and allow Max and me to carry a few."

Jerry debated this for a moment. "Only if you agree to eat some ice cream."

April's eyes scanned the tubs.

Jerry moved in close and lowered his voice to a conspiratorial whisper. "My granny always told me there were no calories on vacation."

April laughed. "I'm not sure my waistline would agree."

"Come on, Lady Bug, live a little." Jerry watched her eyes settle on a tub of strawberry cheesecake. "Atta girl! Come on, what will it be, one scoop or two?"

"One." April giggled. "In a waffle cone."

"Would you like whipped cream, sprinkles, and a cherry with that?" the clerk asked, reaching for a waffle cone.

"Sure." April sighed.

"Atta girl, beautiful!" Jerry said, smiling a triumphant smile. He turned to Max. "What'll it be, kiddo?"

Thirteen-year-old Max didn't have any of her mother's qualms about eating. She pointed to the multi-colored ice cream behind the case. "Superscoop! Two scoops with whipped cream and sprinkles!"

"Hmm, I've never heard it called that. Normally, it's called Superman. Either way, maybe you should make that one scoop," April said as the girl behind the counter handed her a loaded single dip cone. April took a bite, and a portion of the cone fell onto the floor.

"Don't worry, Gunter will eat whatever she doesn't." Jerry grinned, watching the dog lap up the treat.

The clerk handed her a handful of napkins. "Here are some napkins."

April took them and stooped, pretending to clean up the mess. As she did, Gunter eyed her cone.

"Gunter, leave it!" Jerry said firmly.

The clerk stopped scooping and peered over the counter. Not seeing anything, she continued to pack blue, red and yellow ice cream into the waffle cone.

She added whipped cream and sprinkles before handing it to Max and turning her attention to Jerry.

"Two scoops of chocolate in a waffle cone, no whipped cream, and a single scoop of chocolate with whipped cream in a cup for my dog," he said and waited for her reaction. He didn't have to wait long.

"Dogs can't have chocolate," she said, rinsing her scoop.

"It's okay, my dog is imaginary," Jerry replied.

"He's lying. It's his way of getting more ice cream," April said when the clerk looked over the counter at her.

The clerk didn't look impressed. "Should I just give him three scoops?"

April shook her head. "No, we like to humor him. Just give him what he asked for."

Jerry took his packages to the small bistro table in the front corner of the shop and returned for his ice cream. He thought about setting the cup on the floor but saw the clerk watching him and took it to the table instead. He set the cup on the chair and stood, blocking the woman's view while Gunter made short work of the tasty treat. It wasn't that he was worried about her seeing Gunter; it was obvious she couldn't, but he didn't want her to question why the contents disappeared. Gunter nosed the paper cup to the floor and began pushing it with his tongue. Jerry hurried to collect it and toss it in the trash. He saw April watching and laughed a hearty laugh.

She arched an eyebrow. "What's so funny?"

"It just occurred to me that if not for Max having the gift, you would have sent me packing ages ago." His smile faded when a frown knitted her brows as she considered his words, and he knew he was right.

"Boy, you two are lucky you have me," Max said, easing the mood.

"We sure are," April agreed.

Jerry nodded his agreement, but the thought stayed with him. Of all the people in the world, why April? Had the universe known to pair them so that April would understand his gift? Or was it so that he could help her understand her daughter's gift? Either way, he knew it wasn't a fluke, and the knowledge helped firm his decision to ask her to marry him.

April tapped him on the shoulder. "Where'd you go?"

"What do you mean? I'm standing right here."

"Your body may be here, but your mind was a million miles away," she told him.

"Fudge."

"Excuse me?" April replied.

"I was thinking about fudge. The Fudge Kitchen is just around the corner. As soon as we're done, we'll go get some."

April's eyes bugged. "Jerry McNeal, are you trying to make me fat?"

"No calories on vacation, remember!" Jerry looked to see Gunter watching him with a dribble of drool easing from the corner of his mouth. He held out his cone, which the dog eagerly accepted.

April looked up from her conversation with Max and saw him standing there empty-handed. "You already ate your cone?"

Jerry nodded to Gunter. "I may have had a little help."

April looked toward where he had nodded. "Is he watching me?"

"Yep," Jerry said, confirming her suspicions.

"Sorry, boy. When I get the chance to eat ice cream without calories, I'm going to eat every single bite."

"Me too," Max agreed.

"See what you started?" April said, looking at Jerry. "It's a good thing we've taken up kickboxing. Though if we keep eating like this, we might need to add to the routine."

"Bunny said she'll teach us water aerobics after we get the pool," Max replied.

That Bunny intended to hang around that long was news to Jerry. "I thought you were going to help her figure out why she is here."

Max shrugged. "She claims she doesn't know."

"You believe her?" Jerry asked.

"I'm not sure. When I ask about her life and her family, she gets sad. I think she's staying around because she likes us. She likes Granny too."

"Look on the bright side," April said. "She's

pretty self-sufficient. She may be forgetful, but it's not as if we have to add on another guest room."

"It's really snowing!" Max said, peering out the window.

April frowned. "We should get going. These shoes are not made for walking in the snow, and I know you still wanted to stop by the fudge store."

"If you two want, you can wait here, and I'll go get the Durango," Jerry offered.

"Do you really think I'd have you walk all the way to the hotel by yourself just so that we don't have to walk in a little snow? Not going to happen," April said firmly.

Jerry started to zip his jacket but decided against it, knowing if the snow let up, they'd be ducking in and out of warm stores on the way back. With his hands full, it would be too hard to zip and unzip the jacket each time. He grinned and collected the bags. "Walk with me, ladies. We'll take our loot and head back to our castle!" Jerry's playful mood evaporated the moment he stepped outside, took in his surroundings, and tested the feel of the air, which felt heavy and full of electricity.

"I didn't think we were supposed to get this much," April said, coming up beside him.

Max's voice held an edge. "Jerry, something feels off. Hey, why is Gunter wearing his vest?"

Jerry looked to see Gunter sniffing the air. At the sight of the vest, he looked back at the ice cream shop while surveying the area for threats. *Easy, McNeal; this isn't the time to panic.* While he wanted to tell April and Max to go back inside, he was wearing his pistol and knew the safest place for them would be with him. "I think we can wait until tomorrow for the fudge. Let's head back to the hotel," Jerry said, fighting the urge to throw down the packages and tell them to run.

April and Max fell beside him, with Gunter leading the way. They'd walked about a block when the sky grew bright, and a boom echoed through the town. Gunter growled as April fell to the ground. *The dream! It's coming true. Gunter, watch Max!* Jerry dropped the packages and covered April with his body.

"Jerry! I can't breathe!" April's words were forced.

He held her tight, afraid to move, as he didn't want to see what the explosion had done to her. *I'm not worried about her looks; just please, God, don't let her die!*

Hands took hold of his shoulders, attempting to pull him away. Jerry elbowed himself free. The hands took hold once more, firming their grip and pulling him to his feet. Jerry turned and swung at his attacker, who caught the punch with his bare hand. Before Jerry could react, the man grabbed hold of his jacket, pulling it up so that he couldn't move his arms. April was hurt, and all Jerry could think of was getting to her as he struggled to free himself. Gunter's howl breached the recesses of his mind. Jerry blinked. The man eased his grip and backed away as April moved in front of him.

There was no blood. No mangled face. Only a furrowed brow and tears. "Are you okay?" April's voice was edged with fear.

"I thought… there was an explosion." Fear swept over him. Had he imagined it? Gunter moved up beside him, leaning in and giving him support. Jerry's fingers found the K-9's fur and felt the vest. He looked at April and saw her blinking back tears and suddenly wondered if he'd been protecting the wrong person. "Max?"

"I'm here," Max said, stepping into view.

It didn't make sense. "The explosion," Jerry repeated.

"Thunder snow," April told him. "I looked up when I saw the flash. I guess I lost my balance. The next thing I knew, you were on top of me, and I couldn't breathe."

The dream, the explosion – he'd acted a fool all because of a freak winter thunderstorm? As the implications hit him, Jerry began shaking with a mixture of relief and foolishness. He remembered the hands pulling him off. Surely he hadn't imagined that. He scanned the area and saw Carter leaning against a building across the street. The man saw him looking and gave the slightest nod. Jerry returned the gesture and turned back to April once more. "I thought…"

She raised her hand and placed her finger on his lips. "I know."

He took her hand, kissed her palm, and placed it alongside his face. "I'm..."

April firmed her jaw and shook her head. "Don't do it, Jerry. You can apologize for a lot of things, but don't you ever say you're sorry for trying to keep us safe."

That she hadn't backed away from his latest bout of PTSD spoke volumes. That she hadn't taken Max and run off in the other direction meant more to him than she would ever know. "I love you, April."

She allowed her fingers to caress his face. "I love you too, Jerry."

"Oh, man," Max said, pulling their attention.

"What's wrong?" April asked.

"Susie's in Saginaw. She just sent me a text that said she was there for some kind of convention, and she wants to come to Port Hope to see us, but we're not there."

Great, he'd summoned the cavalry for a freak winter storm. He'd wasted her time and everyone else's. Okay, maybe not Carter's. If not for him, he might have actually smothered April while trying to save her. Carter's cover had been blown. Then again, April hadn't mentioned seeing the man. Still, it was time to call Fred and have everyone stand down.

Jerry kept his expression unreadable. "Maybe next time, kiddo."

"Nonsense," April said. "Saginaw isn't that far. Tell her we're in Frankenmuth and see if she wants to come hang out here."

Max typed the message on the phone. "I told her where we're staying and what room we're in. Maybe she can get something close."

"Probably real close," Jerry agreed as he stooped to pick up the packages. As he did, he realized the stupidity of his earlier actions. In trying to be a neanderthal, as April had so elegantly put it, he'd managed to leave them all vulnerable. If he'd have needed his pistol, he wouldn't have had a free hand to draw it. *McNeal, for being a smart man, you sure can be stupid.*

As if reading his mind, April held out her hand. "Please let us help carry them."

Jerry handed her a couple of bags. April rewarded him with a smile.

"If Susie is coming, does that mean I don't have to go to the auction tomorrow?" Max asked as they walked to the hotel.

"I thought you were looking forward to it," Jerry replied.

April laughed. "That's before she experienced the water slides."

"Yeah, I guess a waterslide kind of trumps an auction in a kid's eyes," Jerry agreed.

"Does it mean I don't have to go?"

The hairs on the back of Jerry's neck prickled. "How about we leave that to Susie?"

"Yeah, she might not have a bathing suit. Plus, you said she's been at a convention. She might be too tired to follow you around," April told her.

"She doesn't have to stay. I'm thirteen. It's not like I even need a babysitter," Max countered.

"We will discuss it when we get back in the room. It's been a long day, and we're all tired."

"Is something wrong?" Jerry asked when April looked over her shoulder.

"Not if you're not picking up on anything." She laughed. "It's just that ever since we left Zehnder's, I've had the feeling we're being followed."

Jerry wanted to tell her that Carter was following them and let her know how proud he was of her for listening to her gift of fear, but after his little meltdown, the last thing he wanted was to draw attention to the fact that he might not be the most stable man on the planet.

Chapter Nine

Jerry stepped into the hallway, expecting to see Carter standing in his usual spot. He wasn't there. He double-checked to ensure the door was locked and made his way to the lobby with Gunter at his side. He sat in an overstuffed chair in the corner and texted Fred. > *We need to talk.* Jerry hit send as Gunter sat in a crouched position at his feet, ears alert. The phone rang. He swiped to answer and placed the phone to his ear. "I'm assuming Carter filled you in," Jerry said, forgoing the formalities.

"He gave me his version," Fred replied.

"There's only one version. I freaked out and nearly suffocated April in the process," Jerry sighed. "Looks like I really screwed up on this one. You might as well send everyone home."

"You're telling me you've been there all day, and

you haven't seen one ghost that needs your attention."

"I might have had a run-in from a spirit of Christmas past, but what does that have to do with anything?"

"Because dealing with spirits is your job. Listen, McNeal, your ego may be bruised at the moment, but I've never known you to ask for help where it wasn't warranted."

Jerry wanted to agree with the man, but he didn't feel very agreeable at the moment. "There's a first time for everything."

"Be that as it may, my agents are already in place, and I prefer to keep them there for the time being. What's on your agenda for tomorrow?"

"April wants to go to an estate auction."

"I thought you like to shop. Why don't you sound happy about that?" Fred asked.

"I am, but Max doesn't want to go. She thinks that since Susie is coming, we should let them hang out at the pool and waterslide."

"Again, I don't see the problem," Fred said. "It's still cold in both Michigan and Maine. I've seen pictures of the inside of your hotel. I'd think hanging out by the pool would be a welcomed retreat."

"I'm pretty sure I'm just out of sorts, but as soon as she said she wanted to stay, I got a hit. At the same time, if she were to stay here with Susie, I would only need to keep an eye on April."

"The fact you are still getting hits lets me know I'm right in keeping my guys in play. Listen, if the girl wants to swim, let her swim. Susie will see that she's safe, and just to be sure, I'll put a second set of eyes on them."

At the mention of a second set of eyes, Jerry felt his shoulders relax. "I wouldn't say no to that."

"Good, consider it done. And, McNeal, don't beat yourself up about that incident in town. Carter said if he'd been in your position, he would have reacted the same way."

Only Carter hadn't reacted that way. While Jerry had been gripped with a PTSD episode, Carter had remained clearheaded enough to pull him off of April before he'd suffocated her and somehow managed to do it without being seen. "Roger that, sir." Jerry ended the call and blew out a sigh when he saw Carter heading his way. Great, just what he needed. Gunter rose as the man approached and gave a low growl, causing Jerry to take a closer look. He noted a shadow following the man. Though the spirit hadn't fully revealed itself, it was clear Carter wasn't alone. If the man knew of his ghostly tagalong, he didn't show it.

"Got a minute?" Carter said when Jerry started to get up.

Jerry remained seated and tried to get a bead on the apparition without letting the spirit know he could see it.

Carter took the chair across from him. Gunter remained in place but leaned into Jerry's legs as if offering moral support while both watched the spirit.

"I didn't come here to gloat," Carter said before Jerry had a chance to speak.

"Seems like a missed opportunity," Jerry replied.

Carter crossed his arms in front of his chest. "You're a hard man to figure out, McNeal."

"How's that?"

"The cockiness is to be expected, you being a Marine and all, but at the end of the day, we are all on the same team here."

"Maybe I don't appreciate you disrespecting those I care about. Appreciating the female form is one thing, but being a pig about it and getting distracted when you are supposed to be working is another thing altogether."

Another chuckle.

"What's so funny?"

"I've been shadowing you and the ladies all afternoon. I've watched you eat more than I would have thought humanly possible and shop as if you've recently won the lottery," Carter replied. "I can tell you exactly what each of you ate, what you purchased, and the descriptions of everyone who has come within a few feet of both April and Max since you've arrived."

Jerry started to remind the man it was his job and ask if he was looking for a medal, but he decided against it, knowing it would only lead to a puffing of the chest. "And yet here you are."

Carter glanced at the enclosed dining room that set just off the lobby. "A man's got to eat."

"And yet here you are," Jerry repeated.

"There are eyes on the room, and I'm going to eat. I just saw you sitting here and wanted to get something off my chest."

"Go on."

Carter uncrossed his arms and leaned forward, keeping his voice low. "I was sent here to do a job. My orders are to watch April and Max. While I may have let my mouth run a bit earlier, I've been doing my job since even before you arrived. I've checked out the comings and goings in the hall and made sure everything is as it should be. I can't help it that April looks smoking hot in a bikini, but at the end of the day, whether she's wearing a coat, a bikini, or a burlap sack, putting eyes on her is my job, and we both know you'd be even more irritated if I weren't keeping them in my sights. Am I right?"

"You're not wrong," Jerry agreed.

Carter looked at his phone when it buzzed then returned it to his pocket. "That was the boss letting me know I'm going to be on you and April tomorrow. Is that going to be a problem?"

"Who do they have with Max?"

Carter raised an eyebrow. "You know that's on a need-to-know basis. If I were you, I'd relax. I've worked with Jefferies for years and can attest that the man is better than good at his job. The people on his team, yours truly included, are some of the most highly trained in the country."

Jerry jumped at the chance to learn more about his boss. "What do you know about Jefferies?"

"Enough."

"Come on, Carter. You said it yourself. We're on the same team."

"Jefferies worked his way up in the ranks. A few years back, he made a bid to put together a special task force that deals with things most people can't wrap their head around."

"Do you know what those things are?"

"I've heard a few things. Then again, you'd probably know more about that program than me since you're in it. So tell me, what is your part in all of this?" Carter settled back into his chair as if he actually expected Jerry to answer.

"As you said, things are on a need-to-know basis." Jerry saw a fleeting frown cross Carter's face. *Come on, McNeal, do the right thing. You know the guys on the team have to know what you're capable of.* "Do you know what it is I do?"

Carter nodded. "I know what they say you can do."

"Be a little more specific," Jerry urged.

"They say you can see and speak to ghosts."

"Spirits," Jerry corrected. "But it probably

doesn't matter since it's apparent you don't believe."

"I am more of a science man. If I can see it and feel it, then I'm capable of believing it," Carter said, looking about the lobby. "Let me guess, you're about to tell me I have a spirit attached to me."

Jerry focused on the spirit. *If you have something to say, now is the time.* The spirit faded in and out before completely disappearing. Jerry shook his head. "Nope."

"Good, I was afraid you would turn out to be one of those kooks who think they need to prove themselves to everyone."

"I'm not, but just so we're on the same page, don't go calling for a psych consult if you see me talking to someone you yourself can't see," Jerry replied.

"In my line of work, seeing someone talk to themselves would be a mild day."

"Oh, I never said I would be talking to myself." Jerry smiled.

"Yeah, no need to worry. It's in your file."

"What is?"

"That if you are talking to yourself, we are not to interfere unless it looks like you're under duress."

Great, the whole team probably thinks I'm a nut job. Jerry decided it best to let the comment lie. "Hey, I wanted to thank you for what you did out there."

"Just doing my job."

"Yeah, but if I hadn't…"

Carter cut him off. "Have you ever even heard of thunder snow before today?"

Never. "Didn't even know it was a thing until a couple of hours ago," Jerry admitted.

"I've heard it a couple of times, and it still made my skin crawl. The only reason I didn't go into panic mode was that I'd had an alert to the possibility of it a few minutes earlier. Listen, that your gal fell at the exact moment would have set most people off. Add in the PTSD, and I can only imagine what was going through your mind."

Jerry studied the man to judge his sincerity and decided he was on the up and up. "Thanks, man."

Carter smiled a victory smile. "See, that wasn't so hard now, was it?"

Jerry thought about telling Gunter to bite the man but decided not to since Fred was trying to keep the dog's existence under wraps. Instead, he pushed from his chair with a nod to Carter. "Go get something to eat. I'm heading back upstairs, so take your time."

Jerry bypassed the elevator and raced Gunter up the stairs. As they reached their floor, Jerry saw a man with a rolling ladder working on an overhead light at the end of the hall. Since the man was built like a linebacker, Jerry thought it safe to assume he belonged to Fred's team. He'd just pulled out his hotel card when the door across the hall opened and

Susie stepped out. Wearing a sleeveless black sweater that hugged her curves and loose-fitting slacks, she had her jacket draped over her left arm.

Jerry looked her up and down and made a mental note to give Carter an apology. Anyone with any appreciation for a well-sculpted human form would have to be blind not to appreciate how good the woman looked. He motioned her down the hall toward the elevator so they could talk without being overheard. "Looking good, Richardson," he said once they were out of earshot of the rooms.

Susie grinned. "Put your tongue back in your mouth, McNeal."

Jerry reached and gave Gunter a pat. "I think that goes for you too, fella."

"The dog's not the one drooling," Susie replied.

That Susie could see the dog came as no surprise. It was the main reason Fred had asked her to join the team. Jerry eyed the suitcase. "Looks like you're just getting into town, but we both know you've been here for a couple of days. It's snowing pretty good out. You might want to make mention of the road conditions coming into town."

Susie nodded. "Did you hear thunder earlier? It scared the crap out of me."

"We heard it, but you might not want to mention that unless Max or April does."

Susie frowned. "Problem?"

"Let's just say I wasn't expecting it." Jerry blew

out a disgusted sigh. "Been out of the Marines for over a decade, and I still can't live a normal life."

Susie nodded her understanding. "If it makes you feel any better, I reached for my gun."

Jerry smiled. "Maybe a little. Come on, we'll let April and Max know you're in town. Oh, and just so you know, Max is planning on bailing on us tomorrow if she can convince you to stay here and hang out at the pool with her."

"If you're trying to piss me off, you're going to have to do better than that. Don't you worry about Max, I have no problem getting paid to hang out at the pool all day." She reached a hand to his arm to stop him. "Do you know where the threat is?"

"I don't even know if there is a threat," Jerry replied. "I tried to tell that to Fred, but he insists on keeping you guys here."

Susie let go of his arm. "Have you seen the pool area?"

"Yes."

"Okay, then do us all a favor and stop trying to get us sent home. We've had strong internet, a soft bed and room service. This is the sweetest gig any of us has had in months."

Jerry frowned. "I thought you wanted to be a mortician. Just how many assignments have you been on?"

"A few, and I am. But come on, I live in a small town in Maine; it's not like I'm overrun with people dying to see me. It was a joke, McNeal; you really do need to lighten up."

"I'll lighten up when I know my family is safe," Jerry replied.

"They're safe," Susie said. "You know I love both April and Max and will do everything in my power to keep them that way."

Jerry looped his arm through hers. "Thanks for having my back, Richardson."

She turned to him. "You had mine first, McNeal. If it weren't for you, I'd still have my hair dyed black and be afraid of my shadow. You may not realize it, but you saved me. You and Gunter always remind me of Lassie going from town to town helping people."

Jerry laughed.

"What?" Susie asked.

"I used to watch that show with my grandmother."

"Good, then you know that sometimes even the hero needs a hero." She nodded toward the man at the end of the hall, who was still pretending to work on the light. "Enjoy your family time, and let us do our job."

"Yes, ma'am," Jerry replied.

Chapter Ten

Jerry woke to the sounds of hushed whispers. He opened his eyes to see two women standing over his bed.

"Good, you're awake."

I'm not awake. Go away, he said without speaking.

"I'm Elke, and this is my sister Lina. We were told you can help. You are Jerry McNeal, aren't you?"

"Mr. McNeal is sitting in the hallway. Go bug him."

"The man outside stared through us like we weren't even there," Lina replied.

"Mr. McNeal, it is imperative we speak to you, and we won't go away until you hear what we say." Elke's tone left no doubt she meant what she said.

Jerry looked at the clock, which read 2:45, and blew out a sigh as he swung his legs over the side of the bed.

"Is everything okay?" April's voice was heavy with sleep.

"Yep. Just have a couple of ladies who need to talk to me."

"Alive or unalive?" April asked groggily.

"Long gone," Jerry assured her.

"Okay, have fun," April said, rolling in the opposite direction.

"Not likely," Jerry replied. It was too late. He could tell by April's breathing she'd already drifted off to sleep. He pulled on his pants and addressed the women. "Wait for me in the hall."

Both women disappeared without another word. While Jerry wanted nothing more than to go back to bed, he knew if he didn't see what they wanted, they would be back. He pulled his t-shirt over his head, slipped into his shoes, and plucked his room key, cell phone, and Bluetooth earpiece off the table before stepping into the hall.

The man who'd been changing the lightbulb earlier sat in a chair at the end of the hall. Jerry raised his hand to acknowledge the man before turning in the opposite direction. Not wishing to disturb anyone, he took the stairs to the lobby, which was quiet given the early hour. Not wishing to be overheard, he went into the dining room, which was a glass-enclosed atrium that also housed the adult-only pool. While the room was empty, the glass walls prevented true privacy. He walked to a corner table, removed his cell phone from his pocket, and placed the earpiece in his ear. He pulled out a chair and called to the empty room as he sat. "Hello? Anyone here?"

Gunter appeared, smiling a K-9 smile. The dog wagged his tail.

"It's good to see you too, boy."

Taking that as an invitation, Gunter lifted one leg, then another, until he'd managed to ease the front half of his body into Jerry's lap.

This was new. While he'd seen Houdini do this to both April and Max, the pup's father had never sought out gratuitous affection. Jerry raised an eyebrow. "Really, dog?"

Gunter wagged his tail and answered with a K-9 kiss.

As Jerry sat scratching the dog behind his ears, he wondered if the spirits were going to show. He got his answer a few moments later when the rustling of skirts announced their arrival even before they showed themselves. "Okay, boy, time to go to work." Jerry blocked the spirits from hearing his thoughts and motioned Gunter down.

Gunter placed his paws on the ground and stood between Jerry and the women, who now regarded the dog with furrowed brows.

Jerry regarded both women. While they spoke with German accents, their dresses were not anything like the Dirndl dresses he'd seen in town. While he wasn't an expert, he thought their clothes were more in line with what early 20th-century American women wore. Each woman wore a single string of pearls with their hair piled high on their head. "You wanted to talk, now talk," Jerry said, pulling their attention away from Gunter.

"Sister and I have a problem," Elke said.

"Which is?"

"We don't want them to sell our picture," she replied.

Okay, this is a new one. "I'm afraid I'm not following you."

"You are Jerry McNeal, aren't you?" Elke asked.

Jerry nodded. "I am."

Elke looked him up and down. "She said you can understand us."

It was too early in the morning for this. "Listen, I can hear you just fine. I just don't know what picture you're talking about or who I'm supposed to stop from selling it."

"Oh, well, it isn't really a picture. It's not like a photograph anyway. It is a frame with sentimental belongings inside, and we do not wish to sell it."

"You're dead. It's not really up to you what happens to your belongings." Jerry looked at each spirit in turn. "You do know you are dead, don't you?"

"Of course, we know," Lina told him. "We also know you are alive, so it is up to you to stop the sale."

"Why does it matter?" Jerry asked.

"I told you," Elke's tone was short and sounded like a woman who was used to getting her way. "The thing has sentimental value."

"Okay, let's try this again. I understand the thing meant something to you when you were alive, but you can't take things with you. Unfortunately, that means your next of kin are free to do with them as they choose. This means they can decide to keep your belongings, throw them away, or even sell them."

"That's the thing," Lina interjected, "the person selling them is not our next of kin."

Jerry rolled his neck. "Where is this relic?"

"Just up the road. Come on, we'll show you."

"It's nearly three in the morning," Jerry reminded them.

Both women stared at him without blinking.

"I'm not going anywhere." Jerry crossed his ankles to drive home the point.

"But you're Jerry McNeal."

Jerry sighed. "You keep saying that like it should mean something."

"It does. Mrs. Emerson told us…"

Jerry cut her off. "You're telling me Bunny told

you to come find me?"

Both women bobbed their heads.

"Yes, we met her this afternoon. She was in the barn when they were setting up the estate auction. She is a lovely woman, though we wouldn't have the nerve to leave the house dressed as she does. Especially with our hair painted up like that," Lina replied.

"The auction isn't until tomorrow," Jerry said dryly.

"Which is why we are here tonight. If we waited until tomorrow, it would be too late."

Jerry was glad he hadn't sat next to the wall, as he would have been tempted to beat his head against it. "Bunny. Show yourself."

Instantly, she was there. Dressed in a nightgown, she had white cream slathered on her face. Jerry resisted the urge to remind the woman she was dead.

She worried her hands together. "Are you mad, Jerry? You sound mad."

Before Jerry could answer, Elke's energy grew dark and she wagged a finger in Bunny's face. "You said he could help us."

Bunny swallowed. "A little help here, Jerry."

Jerry started to tell her it was her mess and to figure it out for herself when Gunter growled. *Oh, for Pete's sake.* "How exactly am I supposed to stop them from selling the heirloom?"

"You're Jerry McNeal," Elke replied.

Jerry looked at Bunny. "What exactly did you tell them?"

"Only that you can fix things." She turned to the sisters. "It's not a lie. I've seen him do it."

Jerry sighed. He'd read the info on the auction, which was touted to be a multi-family estate auction. "I'm assuming they are auctioning off lots of items that have been in your family for years. What is so important about this picture?"

"Allow me, Sister." Lina closed her eyes and pressed her fingers to her temples.

Instantly, Jerry saw a collage of a fabric quilted into the shape of a flower and a strip of intricately crocheted lace. A handwritten note above the lace carried the words *Love Overflows & Joy Never Ends In A Home That's Blessed With Family And Friends.* The word LOVE trailed vertically down the left side of the frame. "I see it. Now tell me why it is so important."

Lina lowered her hands. "Our family traveled to America from Germany in 1850. It was a long trip that was both harrowing and exhilarating. It took us seven weeks to arrive in New York City. We came in through Castle Gardens, which is where they brought people before Ellis Island opened up, and waited in long lines for them to deem us healthy enough to enter, but we did not care, as so many had died on the way over.

"Once processed, we were allowed to walk the

streets and visit the markets. The first thing our mother purchased was enough fabric to make each of us sisters a dress. There were eight of us, all girls, and we had all survived the trip to America. So, Momma took us by the hand one by one and told us to pick our fabric for the dress; of course, she only spoke German, so she said it in the language of our homeland.

"We thought she would make us traditional Dirndl dresses, but instead, she made us simple frocks. While each dress was the same pattern, they were different because none of us chose the same color fabric. Mother said it was because we were each different and were now allowed to bloom. She also bought fabric to make the traditional dress, but we never forgot how special we felt in those simple dresses."

"Later, we discovered she'd kept those dresses and had cut fabric from each to sew into a small lap quilt, which she used to cover herself with our memories when we'd grown and went out on our own. Momma was working on the spider lace a week before she died. It was supposed to be a doily, but she passed before finishing it. She was 94 years old when she died in 1892. All of us sisters went on to marry well, but we never forgot our roots and our family's simple beginnings when we first came to America."

I wonder what happened to the other sisters?

Instantly, Jerry was glad he'd blocked them from gleaning his thoughts. The last thing he needed was six more women trying to get him to do their bidding. "Why doesn't anyone know how special the collage is?"

"It first left the family after my granddaughter died," Elke replied. "We tried to stop it from selling, but no one could hear us. The others finally gave up the crusade and went on to the afterlife, leaving Lina and me to be the watchers."

Jerry started to ask if that meant they'd been haunting the wall hanging. He got his answer when Elke continued her story.

"Thankfully, it was purchased by a nice lady who hung it in her sewing room."

"She was such a nice woman," Lina agreed. "Never uttered a foul word. Sister and I enjoyed our time there. Then, after she died, her husband gave it to their neighbor with a bunch of other things he didn't want. That woman kept it in a box for a while before stumbling upon it in her attic."

"It was so dreadfully hot up there." Elke now held a fabric fan that she used to cool herself. "She donated it to a charity auction, and eventually, it ended up here."

"The problem," Elke said, "is we've done some research, and there are three people who are terribly interested in our picture, and none of them will do."

"Why won't they do?" Jerry asked.

"Because," Elke continued, "Sister and I don't want to go with any of them. Mr. Luke smokes like a chimney, and even if that weren't the case, he only wants it for the frame. Mrs. Malone is only after Mother's lace because she thinks it will look nice in the dollhouse she's decorating, and Mrs. Stine wants to hang it in the bathroom of her lake house. Can you imagine the smell?"

"Maybe it's time to let it go?" Jerry suggested. "I know it meant something when you were alive, but they are just memories of this world. You can leave and leave those memories behind."

"Like it's that easy," Elke said. "We will not let it out of our sight until we see it returned to the family. We just don't know how to find them. Until then, we will be the watchers."

"Indeed," Lina agreed.

Jerry wanted to argue the point, but he was tired. He almost wished it did belong to one of the families hosting or managing the sale, as it would be somewhat possible to reason with them and tell them why the piece meant so much. "Maybe if I tell them why the piece is so important, the seller can use the information to get other bidders?" Jerry said, echoing his thoughts.

"That will not solve our problem." Elke turned to Bunny, who'd been surprisingly quiet. "You told us he would help us."

"I'm trying to," Jerry said, drawing her attention.

"It's three in the morning. The sale is in a couple of hours, so precisely, how would you like me to fix it?"

"Find us a better place to live until we can see it returned to the family," Lina replied.

"Oh, I know," Bunny said, clapping her hands together with the delight of a child who'd just solved a puzzle. "Jerry can buy the collage and you can come live with us! He's building a new house, so there'll be plenty of room."

Jerry started to remind Bunny that she did not actually live with him but knew that would only serve to create another argument, as the woman had attached herself to his family and refused to talk about why she hadn't left. He looked at Gunter, who crouched next to him, listening to the proceedings, and it suddenly occurred to him he'd gone from helping spirits to operating a boarding house for wayward souls. Not that he minded having the dog around; on the contrary, Gunter filled a void he never knew existed.

"I suppose it could work," Elke said. "At least he can see and hear us."

"Yes, it's so rude when the living ignore us," Lina agreed.

"Then it's settled. You ladies will just love Max and April."

Jerry felt a tug of anxiety at the mention of April and Max. He was supposed to be protecting them, and here he was downstairs negotiating with a group of spirit terrorists. *Okay, McNeal, don't be so dramatic. Just agree to the buy and you can deal with the fallout later.* "Fine. Find me tomorrow and I'll bid on your keepsake. For now, I'm going back to my room. By myself," he said when everyone started to follow. He looked at Gunter when the dog hesitated. *Come on, boy, you know you're family.*

Gunter sprang from his crouch and followed Jerry back to his room.

"How did it go?" April asked when Jerry slipped back into bed.

"We're going to need a bigger house," Jerry said, snuggling up behind her.

Chapter Eleven

Jerry heard the door click and opened his eyes to see April coming into the room. Fully dressed in jeans and a sweater, she held his coffee thermos, which meant she'd been downstairs. Great, not only had he slept in, he'd not even heard her leave the room. The only thing that gave him comfort was the fact that Gunter had followed her into the room. She closed the distance and wiggled the thermos in front of him.

He glanced at the clock and saw it was half past seven. "Why didn't you wake me?" he asked, pulling himself up and taking the thermos from her. He thumbed the lid open and inhaled as he took a welcomed drink of black coffee.

"Because you were up half the night chatting with other women." April crawled onto the bed and tucked her legs under her. "Was I dreaming, or did you really tell me we needed to build a bigger house?"

"You weren't dreaming," Jerry said, explaining his meeting with Elke and Lina and the solution they'd reached.

"Let's see, with Gunter, Granny, and Bunny, that now makes five – no, five and a half spirits that frequent our home if we include Houdini, who is only half ghost," April said, using her fingers to count. She laughed. "Our house is haunted, and they haven't even poured the foundation."

"I'm hoping Lina and Elke's stay is temporary," Jerry said, taking another sip.

April frowned. "You're not planning on getting rid of the collage, are you?"

"Yes and no. I was thinking that we could help them get what they want."

"Which is?"

"They want to keep the fabric and lace in the family. So, we just need to track down a relative," Jerry replied. "If we do that, there is a good chance either they will move on or at least move to wherever the fabric ends up."

April's eyes lit up. "Ohhh, let me! I love a good computer hunt."

Jerry leaned in and kissed her. "Baby, I was hoping you'd say that."

April lost the smile as she scanned the room. "They aren't here, are they? Please don't say they are. I don't want them to think I don't want them to stay with us. The last thing I want to do is tick off a spirit."

"Relax, Ladybug. At the moment, we are completely alone."

April's smile returned. "Completely?"

"Yes, ma'am. Gunter came in with you and then went into Max's room," Jerry said, pulling her into his arms.

***

The road leading up to the auction site was lined with cars on both sides, and there was more parking in an empty field across from the barns. The energy surrounding the barns was one of hopeful frenzy, leaving Jerry feeling both excited and anxious since the auctions would be taking place in multiple barns simultaneously. He and April had a list of things they were interested in bidding on – unfortunately, that meant being separated at times. He'd relayed that information to Fred, who'd promised to have someone watching her at all times.

"Are you alright?" April asked when he ran a hand over his head.

"I'm good," Jerry lied. The truth of the matter was he hated crowds and hated that he would have to leave April to bid on a collage he had no interest in other than appeasing the women who'd visited him in the wee hours of the morning. The fact they'd yet to show themselves to him let him know they were probably hanging around the item, discouraging potential bidders. He surrounded himself with the white light to protect himself from picking up unwanted energy as he studied the map April had downloaded, showing the barn numbers and listing the auction times.

"It looks like most of my items are in barn one," April said, looking over his shoulder.

Jerry looked at the list, saw the listing for the marigold carnival glass pedestal punchbowl, and attempted to keep his expression unreadable. It was an exact duplicate of the punchbowl his grandmother had been outbid on when they'd driven to Sevierville years ago. He'd shown the listing to April and told her it looked like the one Granny had desperately wanted. While April had marveled at the piece, she'd quickly moved on, looking at other items. While frivolous, he felt he owed it to his grandmother to at least try to bring it home. Plus, he thought it would be a good engagement gift for April and something they could pass down to Max. He checked the auction time for the punchbowl against the auction time of the fabric and lace, both of which would be held in a different barn than most of the items April was after. As long as things remained on schedule, he should be able to bid on both and secure them in the Durango before meeting up with April.

"I'm going to go in and find a good place to stand," April said, turning to the first of the large red barns.

"I'll walk you over and then see about getting that frame for the ladies," Jerry replied. Jerry smiled when Gunter bumped against his leg as if letting him know he was fully capable of watching over both of them. "Gunter will probably go with me. If you need him, he'll be there."

"Okay."

"You're going to stay in this barn until I come back, right?"

April gave him a long look. "Are you afraid I'm going to get lost?"

"Not if you stay in the barn." Jerry saw Carter hovering near and breathed a little easier.

April pointed across the barn. "There's a post over there. Why don't you just handcuff me to it?"

Jerry smiled.

April laughed. "Oh, no, you don't! Listen, this isn't my first auction. I know what I'm doing and will be fine. Stop being a worrywart and go have fun."

Before he could answer, a man in a dark suit appeared next to April.

"Problem?" April asked when he sighed.

"We have a visitor," Jerry said with a nod to the newcomer. That the dog hadn't growled told Jerry the new arrival didn't pose a threat. "Hang here for a minute so I don't look like a wacko talking to myself. "What can I do for you, Mr....?"

The spirit waved him off. "The name's not important, though if you want to call me something, I guess Purnell will do."

"What can I do for you, Purnell?"

"Actually, it's what I can do for you."

Jerry stopped and rocked back on his heels. "Okay, I'll bite. What can you do for me?"

"I was sent by the committee to ask you to do something about Kris. I can take you to him."

Instantly, Jerry knew he was talking about the Santa look-alike on the bridge. "Is his name really Kris?"

Purnell shrugged. "It's what he insists on being called. Now, the committee doesn't care what his name is. They care about the man giving the town a bad name. He's buzzing around the tourists, making them think the town is full of gnats. He's scaring the horses and even had the audacity to push a young lad off the half-wall near the public restrooms in town. The committee doesn't mind him living here, but if he wants to stay, he will have to stop all the bah humbug."

"Care to fill me in?" April asked.

"The gentleman I'm speaking to is part of a committee who wants to clean up the town," Jerry said, bypassing the details.

April's eyes grew wide. "Spirits have committees?"

"Surprised me the first time too," Jerry replied.

They both looked when the loudspeaker squealed. "Listen, things are starting, and this might take a bit."

April nodded her understanding and gave him a quick peck on the lips. "Go do your thing and come find me when you're done." She turned, making her way through the crowd. Seconds later, Carter followed.

Jerry glanced at Gunter. Though the dog watched April, he made no move to follow. Figuring the dog knew what he was doing, Jerry placed his earpiece in his ear and headed out of the barn, knowing the spirit would keep up.

"Where are you going?" Purnell asked when Jerry headed to the furniture barn. "I thought you were going to see Kris."

Jerry paused outside the barn where the fabric and lace frame were to be actioned. "I will, but I have a couple of things to do first."

"But Bunny said…"

Jerry cocked an eyebrow. "What's Bunny got to do with this?"

"She was at the meeting and told the committee to speak to her Jerry."

Oh, for the love of…easy, McNeal. "I'm not 'her' Jerry, and she doesn't speak for me."

"But you do know her?"

Jerry sighed. "Yes, I know her."

"Good. She's a rather intriguing woman and

speaks so highly of you."

Jerry heard the auctioneer's voice over the loudspeaker. "Listen, I have a few things to do. I promise to speak to Kris and try and settle him down before I leave town."

"The sooner, the better," Purnell replied.

"Before I leave town," Jerry said firmly. The last thing he needed was for the spirit to think he had the upper hand.

Gunter bared his teeth and inched forward.

"Oh my," Purnell said and promptly disappeared.

The second Jerry stepped into the barn, Lina and Elke appeared at his side. He looked for Bunny, but didn't see her, a good thing, as she was not on his good side at the moment.

"There are three before us," Elke said, hooking her arm through his and leading him forward. "It'll go fast, so stay on your toes."

Gunter walked ahead of them, clearing the way as the auctioneer's voice sang out over the speakers. Jerry always wondered what it was people felt to make them move aside.

The sisters stopped and stood on either side of him. Elke pointed to a man with a clipboard standing nearby. "I believe Sister and I have scared the others off, but Mr. Luke might give you a run. The man's been practically drooling over the frame ever since he got here. Lina even caught him trying to bribe the man to allow him to buy it outright."

"I think he would have done it too if Elke hadn't gotten into the guy's mind," Lina said, bobbing her head. Mr. Luke moved closer to the center when the auctioneer repeated the final bid and deemed the item sold. "Oh, get ready, we're next."

Jerry rolled his neck and made a show of tapping the earpiece. "Don't worry. I've got this," he said confidently.

A man brought the frame out and held it up for all to see.

The auctioneer read from the card. "Item number 42 is a nice piece of art with an antique quilt piece and lace estimated to date back to the nineteenth century. Who'll start the bid at a hundred dollars?"

"Ten dollars," Mr. Luke shouted.

"Fifteen," Jerry countered.

"Twenty," called someone from the other side of the room.

"Twenty-five," Mr. Luke said, staying in the game.

"Why aren't you bidding?" Lina asked when Jerry remained silent. Mr. Luke and the other bidder went back and forth, with the auctioneer repeating their bid and asking for more.

"Because it will only drive the bid up. I'll jump in when one of them gives in."

The bid rose to ninety-five, and the woman competing for the piece shook her head.

"Ninety-five, ninety-five, who'll give me a

hundred dollars," the auctioneer sang out.

Elke yanked Jerry's hand up.

"A hundred dollars! Do I hear one twenty?"

Once again, Jerry's hand was lifted against his will.

"Our guy on the right must really want the piece, as it seems he's bidding against himself," the auctioneer said, drawing chuckles from the crowd. He looked at Jerry. "Want to make it one fifty?"

"Only if I have to," Jerry said, crossing his arms so they couldn't be lifted without his consent.

The auctioneer turned his attention to the other man. "Do I hear one fifty?"

Luke hesitated.

"I think we've got him," Elke whispered.

"So do I," Lina agreed.

"One thirty," Luke said.

"One fifty," Jerry countered.

Luke hesitated, then raised his hand once more. "One fifty-five."

Jerry knew Luke's commitment was wavering, as he'd narrowed the gap on his bid.

"Two hundred dollars." The voice was eerily familiar.

Jerry looked to see who'd bid and saw all eyes watching him. For a second, he thought perhaps they were waiting to see if he was going to bid, then it dawned on him that he already had, at least they thought he had, as one of the sisters had managed not only to make herself heard but to offer a perfect rendition of his voice.

"We have two hundred going once, going twice."

The man who'd been vying for the frame shook his head in defeat.

The auctioneer leaned in and pointed the microphone at Jerry. "Sold… unless you'd like to counter your bid."

"I think I'm good," Jerry said, forcing a smile.

Chapter Twelve

Still reeling from the sale, Jerry tucked the 11x14 frame under his arm and hurried toward the glassware barn. By his calculation, he still had about twelve minutes until the punchbowl came up for bid.

"I don't know why you're so upset," Lina said, following after him. "Sister and I couldn't be happier."

Jerry stopped and faced the womanly spirits. "The man was done. Five more dollars at the most."

Elke tsked her disapproval. "What's the big deal? It's not like you didn't have the money."

"That's right," Jerry said coolly. "It was my money. I wouldn't have had a problem going to two hundred or even more if it came to that, but you took the decision away from me. Half the fun in bidding on an auction is going toe-to-toe with another person and watching them back down. That moment when you know you won is the best feeling." Jerry nodded to Gunter and began walking once more.

"So, you're saying you don't feel satisfied," Lina said.

"That's precisely what I'm saying. I didn't win this. I stole it. No, you two stole it. I have half a mind to rip it open and give that man the frame."

"Go ahead," Elke urged.

Jerry stopped once more. "What do you mean 'go ahead'?"

Elke shrugged. "We don't care about the frame; it's not like it's original. We only care about the lace and the quilt piece."

Jerry couldn't believe his ears. "You could have shared that bit of information a little sooner."

"Why, whatever for?" Elke asked.

"Because," Jerry said evenly. "You said the man only wanted the frame, not the contents. If you had told me the frame didn't mean anything to you, I could have approached the man earlier and made a deal to sell it to him. Then we all could have been happy. Heck, I could have given it to him and still come out way ahead."

"We told you he only wanted the frame," Lina insisted.

This was true. "Yes, but you didn't say that you didn't want it."

"Now you're just splitting hairs," Elke huffed.

Gunter looked at him as if to say, *You know I have the power to make them go away.*

While Jerry wanted to take the dog up on it, his conscience wouldn't allow him to. He walked to the glassware barn and stopped just short of going in. "Listen, I'm going in here to bid on a punchbowl, and I do not want any help from anyone. I will do the bidding. I'll decide how much I'm willing to go and when to throw in the towel. Is that understood?"

"It's your money," Elke said.

"Indeed," Lina agreed.

The rules being established, Jerry stepped into the barn. The glassware auction was apparently more popular than the barn he was just in, as it was packed.

A woman with a neon vest stood just inside the door. "Bidding or watching?" she asked as he entered.

"Bidding," Jerry replied.

The woman handed him a red handheld fan with a popsicle stick handle. "If you see something you want, give it a wave."

"Yes, ma'am," Jerry said, moving into the barn. Even with Gunter's help, it was too crowded to get to the center of the barn. Not that it mattered, as they had spotters stationed about the room calling out the bids as the auctioneer called for more. While Jerry disliked crowds, he got caught up in the energy with each piece offered and warmed to the blend of excited anticipation as fans rose and spotters shouted. The bidding ended as the auctioneer shouted sold.

That excitement intensified when two men walked on stage carrying the punchbowl. They walked the perimeter of the stage, carefully displaying the set on an outstretched board. Even from where he stood, Jerry could see the sparkle in the light orange-gold glass. As Jerry took in the shape of the bowl, which rose up and down along the edges in what appeared to be a flower-shaped bloom, he confirmed it was identical to the one Granny had failed to purchase all those years ago. By the time the punchbowl was set on the table next to the auctioneer, Jerry was so pumped up that he was determined to purchase it at any cost. Then again, it might just have been because Granny now stood on stage lovingly peering at the bowl as she ran her ghostly fingers along the ruffled edge of the glass.

The auctioneer held up a card. "Here we have a 1920s Marigold Carnival Imperial glass Hobstar & Flower pedestal punchbowl set complete with six cups. This stunning turn-of-the-century beauty is in excellent condition without any chips or cracks. The iridescent coloring is magnificent and would make a stunning centerpiece on any table. Who'll give me a hundred dollars?"

"Isn't that your grandmother?" Elke asked.

"Yep," Jerry replied.

"She seems really taken with that piece. Aren't you going to bid on it?" Lina asked when Jerry hesitated.

Jerry ignored her, waiting until the initial bidding played out. It was a trick Granny had taught him. With fewer bidders in the fray, it gave one time to see who they were bidding against. Most of the time, it worked, but sometimes, like when she'd tried to win the punchbowl herself all those years ago, the other party won out. In her case, it wasn't her lack of determination that derailed her. It was a lack of finances. Jerry was blessed that he didn't have to worry about that. He didn't have to wait long for the bidding to stall at a hundred and twenty dollars.

The auctioneer studied the room. "One twenty, do I hear one thirty?"

Jerry raised his fan, smiling when one of the spotters relayed his bid. Granny looked in his direction and beamed her approval.

"We have one thirty; who's going to give me one forty? One forty! Do I hear one fifty?"

Jerry raised his fan and continued to do so as the bid rose to three hundred dollars. He couldn't see who he was bidding against, but it didn't matter; he was in it for the long haul.

Granny frowned when the bids continued to rise.

"Uh oh," Lina said over his shoulder. "Your

grandmother doesn't look happy. Maybe she thinks you should stop."

"No, she's just worried about my spending so much." Jerry saw the man next to him raise an eyebrow. He tapped the earpiece, hoping to convince the guy he wasn't talking to himself, and raised his fan once more. A worthy opponent, the person bidding against him raised the bid again. It wasn't long before they topped four hundred dollars, which was much more than the punchbowl's estimated value. Fun was fun, but Jerry wondered at his opponent's resolve and if the person bidding against him had their own agenda. *Gunter, go see if you can get the bidder to reconsider.* Okay, it was a cheap shot to use a ghost to win a bid, but this was for Granny, after all.

Gunter disappeared and reappeared a moment later. Facing him, the dog rose up and placed his paws on Jerry's chest. "Dude. What's your problem? Come on, boy, get down. I don't have time to play. I need to keep my head in the game." Jerry started to raise his fan once more.

"Four forty going once. Going twice," the auctioneer said.

Gunter pawed at his arm.

Jerry felt the punchbowl slipping from his grasp as he pulled his arm away. He started to lift his arm to match the bid and Gunter took the arm in his mouth. When Jerry tried to pull it free, the dog growled. "That's enough," Jerry said, attempting to pull away once again.

Gunter released him.

"Sold for four hundred and forty dollars!" the man said, pointing in the opposite direction. Jerry looked to the stage and saw the men lifting the punchbowl from the table. He sighed in defeat as Granny followed the men from the stage. He considered moving to the pickup zone to lay eyes on the person who'd outbid him but knew seeing them with the punchbowl would sting even more than his being outbid. Securing the frame under his arm, he went in search of April.

***

April felt a moment of guilt as she'd promised Jerry she would remain in the barn until he returned. While she hated to lie to him, she knew the guilt of the moment would pass the second she presented him with the punchbowl she planned on buying for him. She recalled the way his eyes lit up when showing her the bowl and telling of the special memory connected to one that looked just like it. While he took great pleasure in buying things for others, he rarely purchased things for himself. Even in the weeks leading up to Christmas, when she was begging for ideas for something for him, he kept assuring her that Max and she were all he needed to make him happy. She regretted the look of disappointment he'd shown when she'd blocked him from her thoughts and feigned indifference to the piece, but it was the only way she could think of to act that wouldn't let on she planned to buy it for him. She hadn't been sure how she was going to pull it off at first, but things fell into place when he'd told her of the sisters and of his promise to bid on their frame. When she learned the item would not be auctioned off in the same barn as the punchbowl, she knew fate had intervened.

April waited for him to leave the household barn and gave him enough time to get to the furniture barn before making her way to the glassware barn. Sure, he would eventually know she'd fibbed to him, but by then, she could present him with the treasure. Boy, would he be surprised.

As she stepped out into the open, she had the distinct feeling she was being followed. Nothing new, as she'd had the same feeling ever since arriving in Frankenmuth. She looked over her shoulder and saw a man she'd seen hanging around the hotel pool. Okay, kind of weird, but then again, she'd been with Jerry the other times she'd seen him, and he would have said something if he had felt the man was up to no good. She pulled her phone from her pocket, pretending to take a selfie, and took a photo of the man. Feeling silly, she pocketed her phone and decided to put some distance between them. She hurried to catch up to a couple walking in front of her and matched their pace, feeling there was safety in numbers. It dawned on her she would be even safer if Gunter were with her. She thought about willing him to come to her but didn't want to take him away from Jerry in case he needed the dog's help. Jerry hated crowds because of the energy. Perhaps she was just picking up on that. Actually, it made sense, as Savannah had told her she thought her to be empathic. Yep, that had to be it. If it were anything else, both Jerry and Max would have picked up on it. Feeling more confident, she stepped into line and funneled her way inside. She stopped at the table.

A rosy-faced woman wearing a fluorescent vest greeted her. "Bidding or watching?"

"Bidding!" April said, feeling her excitement bubble.

"Good luck," the woman said, handing her a fan.

April moved into the barn, sought out a man who looked like he could handle himself and stood next to him. He looked down at her, and she flashed him a quick smile, then turned her attention to the auction stage. Okay, she'd made contact without looking like she was there to pick up a man. She felt safer already.

Thirty-two minutes after she entered the barn, two men stepped onto the stage carrying the punchbowl. The auctioneer held up a card. Excitement surged through her as he read the description and asked for the first bid.

Someone shouted twenty dollars. Then, the bid rose to forty. April's hand shook as she lifted her fan and jumped into the fray, and excitement continued to race through her each time she countered a bid. The bidding stalled with her hundred-and-twenty-dollar bid. *It's mine. I can feel it.* April blew out a breath to temper her excitement.

The auctioneer studied the room. "One twenty, do I hear one thirty?"

"We have one thirty; who's going to give me one forty?"

"Looks like you have some competition," the man standing next to her said.

Determined not to be outbid, April raised her fan.

The spotter pointed at her, and the auctioneer countered her bid. "One forty! Do I hear one fifty?"

Each time she lifted her flag, someone in the barn raised the stakes. The bids rose to over three hundred. While common sense told her to let it go, she kept telling herself the person bidding against her would quit with the very next bid. Only, the person continued to counter.

"I have three seventy-five; who'll give me four hundred?"

Don't do it, April. She raised her fan.

Her bid was instantly countered at four twenty. Okay, time to throw in the towel. Fun was fun, but this was verging on ridiculous. One more bid, and she was done.

"Four twenty, who'll give me four forty?"

April raised the fan, knowing it would be her final bid.

"I have four forty, who'll give me four fifty?"

Admitting defeat, April turned away from the stage.

"Four forty going once. Going twice," the auctioneer said.

April paused.

"Sold for four hundred and forty dollars!"

April turned back to the stage as the auctioneer pointed at her.

"Looks like you bought yourself a punchbowl," the man standing next to her said, offering her a high-five.

"I most certainly did. My boyfriend is going to be super excited!" April said and slapped her palm to his. She looked past the man and saw the man from the hotel staring. The crowd parted. For the barest of seconds, she thought she saw Randy standing in the crowd. When she blinked, both were gone. She looked over her shoulder several times as she walked to the table to pay.

"You okay, missy?" the man asked when she approached the table. "You look like you've just seen a ghost."

"I'm good," she said, pulling out her wallet and handing him enough cash to cover her bid.

"They are wrapping it in bubble wrap now and

will bring it out in just a moment," the man said, counting out her change.

While she waited, she took out her phone, attached the photo of the man who'd been following her, and sent it to Carrie with a message that read > *Hey, if I disappear, this is the man they are looking for.* She swiped to answer when her phone rang. "I was just kidding."

"Yeah, right. Who is he, and what are we talking, murder or kidnapping?"

"I'm sure I'm just being overly dramatic. It's just that I've seen him a lot since we arrived."

"You think he's following you?"

Yes. Okay, Carrie was already freaked out; no use fueling the fire. "No."

"But there's a chance, which is why you took his picture."

"Maybe."

"Why do I get the feeling there is more to the story than you are telling?"

Because there is. "I thought I saw Randy," April said, trying to keep her voice light.

"Randy's there? Where's Jerry?"

"Randy's not here. My mind is just playing tricks on me. Jerry's in the other barn. He had a ghost emergency."

"Do you want me to release Houdini?"

While she wanted to say yes, it would mean she would have to explain the dog's presence to Jerry.

"No. Seriously, I'm fine. There are plenty of people here. I'm going to go put my box in the Durango and then go find Jerry."

A man in a neon-yellow vest brought out a box and set it on the table. The man who'd taken her money checked the paper and waved her over.

"Nope, kidnapping 101, never go to the car alone," Carrie said.

Carrie was right. Besides, the box had no label, so it wasn't as if Jerry would know what was in it. "Okay."

"I'm serious, and just so you know, if Houdini as much as whimpers, I'm taking off the harness."

"I know you are." April laughed. "That's why I love you. Listen, I've got to go."

"Text me when you find Jerry so I can stop worrying," Carrie said.

"I will." As April reached for her package, her phone rang, showing Jerry's number. Her shoulders relaxed the moment she answered.

Chapter Thirteen

Jerry worked to shake off the disappointment of not having won the auction for the punchbowl. While losing the auction stung, he had already thought of a backup plan for the proposal. He paused outside the barn and called Fred. "I need a Fred favor," he said as soon as his boss answered.

Fred chuckled. "What exactly is a Fred favor?"

"Something only someone with your resources can provide," Jerry said, watching as Gunter sat and scratched an imaginary itch.

"If you are trying to butter me up, it's working. What do you need?" Fred asked.

"I need to borrow a Santa suit for a couple of hours."

"Dare I ask why?"

"I'm going to use it to propose to April."

"Can I give you some advice?"

"You could," Jerry said, "but I'd prefer you not to. Listen, I know it sounds crazy, but this is a Christmas town. I haven't actually been to Bronner's yet, but April seems to think the place magical. What better place to propose?"

Fred chuckled once more. "I can think of a few. Don't worry, I'll find one. How's it going otherwise? Find any ghosts?"

"More like they found me." Jerry looked over at Lina and Elke, who'd yet to leave his side as he told Fred about them and how they'd pressured him into bidding on the frame. While he told of April's promise to help, he left off telling about his failed attempt at the punchbowl. "I guess they'll be with us until we get this sorted out."

"Let me know if April needs any help with the search."

"Will do," Jerry replied. "I'm going to go find April."

"She's not with you?" Fred's voice held a note of concern.

"No, I haven't seen her in close to an hour. I left her in the houseware barn when I went to bid on the frame. Don't tell me Carter lost her."

"No. If he had, he would've checked in."

"Well, all the same, I'm going to go check on her."

"Okay, you sure I can't talk you out of the Santa suit?" Fred asked.

"I'm sure," Jerry replied. "I've watched some videos of the place, and they have a Christmas tree section. I wouldn't imagine that area is very busy this time of year, so it would be the perfect place to ask her."

"It's your show, McNeal. Who am I to stand in the way of your vision? I'll put Carter on the suit and let you know when we have it in play."

"Thanks," Jerry said, ending the call. The moment he stepped into the household barn, he knew April wasn't inside. Jerry looked at Gunter, who stood next to him, sniffing the air. While he knew they could find her, he decided to call her instead.

"Hey." Her voice sounded relieved. "Did you win your bid?"

For a moment, he thought she was talking about the punchbowl, then realized she was talking about the fabric and lace. He glanced at Lina and Elke, who were standing nearby. "Yep. Holding it in my hands as we speak. Going to be crowded on the way home. How about you? Did you get what you were after?"

"I did. Since you weren't back yet, I was going to put it in the Durango."

Instantly, a chill crawled along his neck. The Durango was parked in a field on the other side of the street. "You're at the Durango? I thought you were going to wait for me in the barn?"

"I'm not at the Durango. I had to go to the bathroom. I'll be back at the barn in a moment." This time, her voice held an edge.

"I didn't mean..." Jerry stopped mid-sentence when he realized April was no longer on the other end. Not that he blamed her since he'd just treated her like a child who couldn't be trusted to cross the road by herself. He looked for Gunter, but the dog was nowhere in sight. Jerry relaxed, knowing the dog had gone to her.

Sure enough, April rounded the corner a moment later with Gunter plastered to her left side. She was wielding a box she could barely see over. Jerry hurried to meet them and saw Carter in the distance. The man gave a subtle nod, then headed off in the opposite direction as Jerry held up the frame. "Here, trade me."

April hesitated before handing over the box. "A couple of things are breakable, so don't shake it." She picked up the frame and ran her finger over the glass as she studied the contents. "Oh, how pretty. Just look at the detail on that lace."

"I like her," Lina said.

"She'll do," Elke agreed.

The moment he took hold of the box, he knew exactly what was inside and knew it was she who'd been bidding against him. Not wishing to spoil her surprise, he kept her secret. "Did you get everything you came for?"

"Not everything, but you know how these things are. You win some and lose some," April replied. "How about you? How did you do?"

"I only ended up with the frame. I guess I'm losing my touch."

"Oh, I'm sorry," April said sincerely.

"It's okay; I had a worthy opponent," Jerry said, tightening his grip on the box. "I got the frame, and you got what you wanted, so I guess we'll call it a win. Have you heard from Max?"

"No, she's probably still at the pool. I talked to Carrie for a moment. She said Houdini is doing good."

"That's good," Jerry replied, knowing if April had genuinely enjoyed herself, she wouldn't have had time to reach out to Carrie. He wondered if she was upset that he'd left her alone and truly hoped Fred would come through with the Santa suit so he could make amends. "Where to next?"

"I'm ready to go if you are," April said and looked over her shoulder. "If you don't mind, I think I'd like to go back to the hotel for a bit."

Jerry frowned. Something was wrong, and yet he couldn't pinpoint what it was. "Are you feeling okay?"

She waved him off. "I'm fine. I just want to check on Max."

Jerry did a mental head slap. Of course, she'd want to check on Max.

"Besides," April continued. "I'm pretty sure she's going to want to go to Bronner's with us. She was telling Susie all about it before we left this morning."

Worried Fred wouldn't have enough time to get the suit he'd asked for, Jerry faked a yawn.

"I forgot you didn't get much sleep last night," April said, taking the bait. "Maybe we should take a nap first."

Jerry smiled inwardly, celebrating his victory. He had a plan; now, he just needed to execute it.

***

The door to the hotel room opened, and Jerry stepped into the room. He smiled at her. "Ready?"

"Sure am," April said, collecting her purse. Seeing that Max was okay, then taking a nap and lying nestled in Jerry's arms did wonders to settle her overzealous imagination. Not only was she convinced that she'd allowed her mind to play tricks on her, but she was also glad that neither Jerry nor Max had seen the extent of her foolishness. "Are Max and Susie ready?"

"They're already down in the parking lot," Jerry said, holding the door for her. "I think they're planning on driving separately."

This came as a surprise, as did the sudden apprehension of not having her daughter nearby. She worked to keep her thoughts unreadable. "Did they say why?"

"No. Is it a problem?" Jerry asked.

That he wasn't concerned meant she was overreacting again. April shook her head. "No, I was just curious."

Jerry stopped at the elevator and pushed the button. The door opened immediately, and Jerry pressed the button for the first floor. "I'm pretty sure it has something to do with Susie's rental car. It's a Mustang."

"Yes, that is probably the reason," April agreed.

Jerry grinned. "I guess you're stuck with me."

"That's okay, Mr. McNeal. I don't mind being alone with you."

Jerry raised an eyebrow as his eyes searched the elevator.

"From your expression, I take it we aren't alone?" She laughed. "Gunter?"

"Yep."

She watched as Jerry pointed. Though she could not see him, she took comfort in the fact he was there.

"Not now," Jerry said when the elevator doors opened.

"Not now what?"

"Business."

Since he hadn't received a text or phone call, April knew it to be ghostly business. "I can ride over with Max and Susie if you want."

"NO!"

For a moment, April wasn't sure if he was yelling at her or whoever had just shown up. The fact that he continued to look in the opposite direction let her know it was the latter.

"Give me a moment, and I'll meet you in the lobby," Jerry said.

April was halfway down the hall when she heard someone sneeze. She turned to bless the person and saw the man who'd been following her. She thought about yelling for Jerry, knowing he was within earshot. But what would she say? It wasn't as if she could prove the man was following her. *Think, April. Gunter!* She willed the dog to her. Though she never saw him, she felt something brush against her leg and knew him to be there. Not wanting to turn her back to the man, she stepped out of the way and looked directly at him as he passed, taking in every detail of his appearance.

He smiled as he neared. "Have a good day," he said and continued down the hall.

April followed at a distance and watched as he left the building. Thinking to get his license plate number, she stepped outside and watched as he got into an eggplant-colored SUV with a Santa suit hanging in the back seat. She giggled as the fear left her. *Geez, April, some detective you are. The guy's here to spread holiday cheer, and you've labeled him a...what exactly did you think he was here to do?* She had no answer but knew it was time to come clean to Jerry about her nightmares before she ended up truly freaking out and accusing someone of something they hadn't done.

***

Jerry hated to ask April to wait for him in the lobby, but the spirit standing in front of him was the same one he'd spoken to at the auction barn. While he appeared harmless, the man's energy was concerning; therefore, it was best to get April out of the way before attempting to speak to him. He was just getting ready to speak with the man when Carter slipped into the hallway from the stairs. Jerry pointed in the direction April had just gone. "Careful, she's supposed to be waiting in the lobby."

"Susie is waiting out front. She'll have eyes on her the moment she leaves the building. I'll meet you at Bronner's," Carter said without stopping.

Jerry waited until Carter was out of earshot before addressing the spirit. "I have something to take care of first."

"That's what you said earlier." Purnell's voice was curt.

"This is something different," Jerry told him.

"Word is this is what you do. What could be more important than doing your job?"

Jerry sighed. "If you must know, I plan on proposing to my lady."

"That woman who got off the elevator with you?"

Jerry nodded. "That's the one."

"By all means, catch that pretty gal before she gets away." Purnell stepped aside, motioned for Jerry to pass, and promptly disappeared. The second he entered the lobby, he saw April waiting near the door.

She saw him coming and smiled. "That didn't take long."

"I told him I'll meet with him later," Jerry explained.

April furrowed her brow. "If you need to take care of this, we can wait to go to Bronner's."

"Are you kidding me? I've been looking forward to this all day."

April's eyes lit up. "Me too. You just wait until you see it. No matter how many times you return, you'll always remember the first trip there."

Jerry matched her smile. "That's what I'm counting on."

***

Though the drive only took a few moments, Jerry's palms were sweating by the time they arrived. He checked his pocket for the box and looked to see Max and Susie waiting by the entrance.

April touched his arm. "Humor me a minute."

"Okay."

"Let me go in first."

"I understand if you don't want to be seen with me," Jerry teased.

"I know it sounds silly, but I want to see your face."

Jerry looked in the mirror at Gunter. "Did you hear that, boy? She likes my face."

Gunter yawned his reply.

"What did he say?"

"Silly girl. You know dogs can't talk."

"Yeah, well, they don't normally come back as ghosts either," April said in return.

"Tell that to the dog," Jerry said and winked.

April opened her door. "Just give me two minutes to get in place."

"Yes, ma'am." Jerry opened his door and watched as she walked toward where Susie and Max stood. Halfway to the building, she stopped and stared off into the parking lot for a moment before continuing on her way. Jerry waited until she was inside, then began a slow walk to the building. As the doors to the south entrance slid open, he looked for April. Not seeing her in the lobby, he continued to the second set of doors, and as he walked through them, the magic of Christmas enveloped him. April hadn't exaggerated; holiday music filled his ears as his eyes searched floor to ceiling, taking in life-size decorations, including nutcrackers, reindeer, Christmas trees, and oversized ornaments that overlooked the showroom floor, which had shelved displays along the walls and throughout the center of the room. A total sensory overload, with each piece outshining the next.

Suddenly, April was in front of him, grinning with girlish delight. "Well?"

"It's everything you said it was," he agreed.

April held up her phone. "And I caught it all on video. Come on, we'll start over here and work our way back to the trees."

At the mention of the trees, Jerry was reminded of his mission. He checked his pocket for the umpteenth time since leaving the hotel and looked about for Carter. Not seeing the man, he followed April to the right and into the section of the building that housed the puzzles, stuffed animals, and toys. They found Max and Susie standing at the stuffed animal display, looking over some hand puppets. April called Max over to check out something she'd spied.

Jerry stepped up next to Susie. "How's it going?"

"Great." Susie stuck her hand inside a bear and moved the puppet's mouth. "Max is a terrific kid."

"Any trouble today?"

"Nothing. If Max keyed on anything, she didn't mention it. Fred told me what you're planning."

"Fred has a big mouth."

"I think it's sweet," she said, letting the bear plant a kiss on his cheek.

"Let's hope she agrees," Jerry said, looking over

at April.

"Are you kidding? The woman is head over heels in love with you."

"Do you think I'm pushing my luck with the Santa suit?"

"Every woman wants an engagement to remember." Susie traded the bear for a badger and pointed it toward Gunter. "Isn't that right, boy?"

Gunter wagged his tail, happy to be included in the conversation.

"A simple yes or no would suffice."

"Follow your heart, Jerry. What's the plan? There is a plan, isn't there?"

"Carter is here. I'm going to meet up with him to get the suit and propose to April back at the trees. It would be nice if you could keep her there until I get dressed."

"Absolutely. You have the ring, right?"

Jerry patted his pocket. "I've had it right here since leaving the house."

"That's sweet."

Jerry ran a hand over the back of his neck. In just a few moments, he would get down on a bent knee and propose to his girl.

"You rubbed your neck. Are you nervous?"

"About the commitment, not even for a second. I just don't want to let them down."

Susie smiled. "They already love you, Jerry. The only way you let them down is not making it official."

"What are you two conspiring about?" April asked, coming up behind Jerry.

Jerry sighed an exaggerated sigh. "I guess we're busted. I was just telling Susie about the house we're having built and how I was going to suggest that while we are here, you should pick out your tree."

April's eyes lit up, and suddenly, she was the most Christmassy thing in the building. Jerry knew that was the moment. He started to bend his knee when April looked over his shoulder.

"Max!" she called to her daughter. "We're going to pick out a tree."

Jerry watched as they took off toward the back of the store.

Susie patted him on the back. "Better hurry up and find Carter, or you're going to be upstaged by a tree."

Chapter Fourteen

Never in a million years did April believe she would be able to pick out a tree from Bronner's CHRISTmas Wonderland, and yet here she was doing just that. The problem was that there were so many to choose from. While Max was pushing her to get a colored tree, she leaned more toward traditional. But even then, there were so many choices and styles. "Susie? What do you think of this one?"

"Oh, no, you don't," Susie said, shaking her head. "You're the one who's going to be living with your decision, so you have to decide what is best for you and your family. The question is, will you say yes or no?"

Okay, that was a little weird. April circled the tree once more, then went to look at another that had caught her eye. As she moved around that tree, something red caught her eye. She turned just in time to see a man dressed in a Santa suit talking to Max. Instantly, she recalled the man who'd been following her all day and the red suit hanging in his car. Her mouth went dry. Jerry had told her to follow her instincts, yet since she'd arrived in Frankenmuth, she'd kept pushing the fear away. The man was a predator, and he was making a move on Max. As she stormed toward the imposter, her momma bear instincts kicked in. *Okay, no more playing nice. I'll teach him to mess with my daughter.*

***

Gunter growled.

Jerry looked up as April took a swing at him. He ducked his head out of the way before she could connect the blow. She came in for another punch. He caught her fist in his hand. Tears poured from her eyes as she fought to get free. Finally, it was Max who reached her.

"Mom! Stop fighting with Jerry!"

"Jerry?" April stopped struggling and blinked her confusion.

Jerry pulled down the beard. "Surprise."

Tears poured from her eyes. "I thought you were him." Her voice shook as she spoke.

He didn't have to ask who she was speaking of, as instantly, his mind was filled with images of Carter following after her, watching her, driving past in an SUV with a red Santa suit hanging from the hook over the rear seat. He saw a man wearing that same suit speaking to Max and understood her fury. What he didn't understand was why he hadn't picked up on it.

He heard Max crying, saw Susie trying to comfort her, and realized he wasn't the only one who'd gotten a sudden information dump. While he didn't know the reason for it, he now knew April had blocked them both from reading her. While he didn't know the reason, he knew that if the threat had been real, the consequences could have been dire. Jerry lifted a hand and wiped at her tears with his thumb. As he did, the image of Carter was replaced by an image of Randy standing in the auction barn. He looked at Max and instantly knew April had released that image to him alone.

He pulled her into his arms and whispered in her ear, "Are you sure?"

"I'm not sure of anything at the moment," she whispered in return. "Please don't say anything to Max just yet."

"Max can help."

"No, not with this. You weren't there, Jerry. I don't want her reliving that."

Jerry pulled back and kissed her on the forehead. "Okay."

April blinked as if seeing him for the first time. "Why are you dressed like that?"

Because I was a fool. Jerry kept the thought to himself and forced a smile. "I guess I just got caught up in the Christmas Spirit. I'm going to go change. Gunter and Susie will stay with you. Wait here. I'll only be a moment."

"Okay," April promised.

As soon as he released her, Susie let go of Max, who ran to her mother.

Susie clapped him on the shoulder. "Go. I won't let them out of my sight."

Jerry waited until he was back in the lounge before pulling out his phone and calling Fred. He put the phone on speaker and shrugged out of the red suit.

"McNeal? Tell me she said yes."

"Where's Randy?" Jerry said, cutting to the chase.

"I'll take that as a no," Fred said.

"Where?" Jerry repeated.

"He's in the wind."

"You knew. That's why you refused to pull the team."

"I found out a few days ago before you asked me to check on him. My man admitted to having lost him."

"Why didn't you tell me?"

"I thought we had it under control."

"You didn't," Jerry fumed. "Is that man still on your payroll?"

"For the time being. Once we find Randy, we'll discuss his future with the agency."

"April thinks she saw him at the auction."

"She didn't say anything?"

"I haven't had a chance to debrief her."

"The heck with debriefing her. What does your gut say?"

"That he's here. And if we want to find him, we need to draw him out."

"What do you have in mind?"

"April and I are going to walk around town. Susie will stay with Max at the hotel. I can handle myself, but you make sure someone has eyes on Max and April at all times. Oh, and just so you know, your boy's been made."

"Carter? I already know. He thought she'd made him at the auction but wasn't sure. He saw her in the hotel, and that time, he knew for sure."

"Yeah, well, if she made him, there's a good chance Randy made him too."

"You want me to pull him?"

"Negative. I want whoever you have here to stay with us until we get this guy."

"It's your play, McNeal. You tell me what you need, and I'll see to it."

***

Jerry and April walked hand in hand across the covered bridge that led to town.

"Are you still upset with me?" April asked.

"I'm upset with both of us," Jerry told her. "You for keeping me out, and me for not letting you in. Most couples have a learning phase, but we kind of jumped in with both feet. I get that you don't want to feel like the damsel in distress, but I'm a Marine and a former cop. More than that, I am a man who loves you more than anything else in the world. Like it or not, my job is always going to be to protect you. That means if you need a spider killed, a jar lid loosened, or an ex-husband disappeared, I'm your guy."

"Are you really planning on disappearing him?" April asked.

"Up to him."

"Do you think he'll find us?"

"If he's here, we're going to make it easy for him."

"What if he goes after Max instead? That's what he told me he'd do if I ever left him."

"Max is with Susie."

"I know you said Susie is good, but she's only human."

Jerry smiled. "That's why Granny is there babysitting them both. Any sign of trouble, and she'll call for Gunter."

"What if he comes for us?"

Jerry started to tell April he hoped Randy would make a move on them, as it would give him all the excuse he needed to permanently disappear the man, but it wasn't what she needed at the moment. She was scared and needed to be reassured. "Listen."

"To what?"

"Hear that hum?"

"Yes."

"It's a drone. The person flying it will have eyes on us at all times as long as we remain out in the open. Have you noticed the man on the bike?"

"The one that keeps passing?"

"He's with us, as was the man standing at the Peacock house when we stopped to look through the screen."

"He was old." April's voice was incredulous.

"Makeup," Jerry told her. "The woman with the baby carriage walking behind us is pushing a doll."

April looked off in the distance. "The couple by the water?"

"Are feeding ducks." Jerry laughed. "Not everyone we meet will be with us, but just know not everyone is who they seem."

"I wish you would have told me about Carter."

Jerry chuckled. "I wish you would have told me about Carter."

"I'm not psychic, and my dreams have never come true. I just wanted to have a normal weekend. I didn't know that blocking you from knowing my thoughts would mean blocking me from knowing I was in trouble."

"It's my fault. I know you've been working with

Savannah, but I need to work with you more myself. I would never give you a weapon without teaching you to use it. This works the same way. The scary thing is, if things had gone sideways, Max and I would have spent the rest of our lives wondering how we'd failed you."

"I'm sorry."

"Me too." They crossed the street and continued to River Place Shops. Jerry saw Carter sitting on a brick ledge near the Black Star Farms Winery, pretending to read a brochure. "Look to the right, but don't acknowledge him in case we are being watched."

"Funny, he doesn't look so scary now that I know who he is," April said, averting her eyes once more.

As they continued to walk, Jerry felt a pang of guilt. The pang was replaced by a tingle a few moments later when Gunter growled.

Jerry looked to see the angry spirit in the center of the gravel, standing on the roof of a miniature static display of the bridge he and April had just walked across. The thing that troubled him was he was surrounded by Purnell and a few other spirits urging the man to jump. "Time to go to work."

"Is Randy here?"

"No, it's the spirit I told you about. He seems to have brought friends."

"What do you want me to do?"

"Honestly, if you don't mind, just stand beside

me so people don't think I'm crazy when I start talking to myself." While not the best scenario, he felt better keeping April near than taking the chance of losing focus and having something happen to her.

Purnell looked up as they neared the display. "For someone who just got engaged, neither of you look too happy."

"Didn't happen."

"You didn't ask her?"

"Not yet."

"Why not?"

Jerry rubbed his hand over his head. "Something came up. Now I am here dealing with you guys. So perhaps if I can get you all sorted out, I can still salvage the day." Okay, it was a small stretch of the truth, but if it worked…

Jerry looked at Kris, who was teetering on top of the bridge. "Kris, my name is Jerry McNeal. I know you're upset about something. I'd like to see if I can help."

Kris wagged a finger at him. "Come any closer, and I'll jump."

Jerry crossed his arms and rocked back on his heels, wondering where to start. "Kris, do you know you're dead?"

The spirit's eyes grew round.

"Even if you weren't, that bridge is not more than a foot off the ground. The most you'd get would be a skinned knee."

The spirit faded in and out.

"Hold on, Kris. I can't have you taking off. I'm leaving here tomorrow, so we need to get you figured out."

Kris stepped down from the bridge. "You wouldn't be lying to me, would you?"

Jerry revisited the conversation. "Am I safe to assume you weren't aware you were dead?"

Kris nodded.

"What's the last thing you remember?"

"I'd just graduated from Santa school over in Midland. They train fellows like me to help out the real dude. We're called Santa's cousins and I'd gotten my first gig. Only when I got there, everyone acted like I was invisible. I hung around there for a bit and got more and more depressed. I thought back to when I was the happiest, and it was here. Me and the fellows and a few of the missuses too were brought here on buses. It was all part of the school where we came over on a nice coach bus, five of them actually. Me and the others walked off that bus to a crowd of onlookers who acted like every one of us was the big man himself. I'm telling you, it was magical. Then I come back here, and, in my mind, I'm the same guy, but people here look right through me."

As he spoke, Jerry could feel the spirit's anger ebb. "That's why you were scaring the horses?"

Kris bobbed his head. "When they freaked out, I

knew they could see me. Just like that dog of yours can see me. Watch this." Kris took a step toward Jerry and stopped when Gunter growled.

Kris stopped. "Easy, fella, I was just proving a point. You know, I don't feel so bad now that I know why people were ignoring me."

Jerry lowered a hand to steady the dog and addressed Purnell. "Can he stay?"

"The more the merrier." Purnell looked to the others, who nodded their agreement.

Instantly, the energy in the area cleared.

"Ask her," Purnell urged.

"Not now," Jerry replied. "I want it to be right."

Kris appeared in front of him, his face two inches from Jerry's. "And what if the right moment never happens? I wanted to go to Santa school for years until I was like, okay, now is the time. While I completed school, I never got to feel the joy of making kids smile. Take it from the big man; if you wait, you may never get the chance."

"Is everything okay?" April asked.

"This situation is defused," Jerry said and received a tingle as he watched Gunter walk into a nearby store. "But we might have another problem. Gunter just went into that store."

"Which one?"

"Cats and Dogs," Jerry said, motioning toward the store.

"Do you think he's looking for Randy?" April

asked, following him inside.

"No. I believe our boy lost focus," Jerry said. He pointed to a glass display of homemade doggie treats.

"What's he doing?"

The K-9 had his head pushed through the glass, licking what appeared to be the white frosting of a cannoli. "Eating a cannoli."

April giggled.

"Hey, dog. I hate to break it to you, but you're supposed to be working," Jerry said firmly.

Gunter groaned and pulled his head back through the glass. The hairs on the back of Jerry's neck stood on end when he saw the dog was now wearing his K-9 police vest.

"Stay behind me," Jerry said. Pulling out his phone, he sent Fred a message. > *He's near.*

As Jerry pocketed his phone, Randy stepped into the doorway, brandishing a pistol.

Before Jerry had time to react, Gunter sailed through the air and hit the man square in the chest, knocking him to the ground.

Gunter hovered over him, snarling, as Carter and the others moved in.

"Glad to see you could make it," Jerry said.

"Jefferies told us to make sure the charge would stick," Carter said. Oblivious of the dog, he hoisted Randy up. "Dude. Why'd you have to go and trip over your own feet? You made this too easy," Carter said, slapping on the cuffs.

"What do you mean trip over my feet? That dog attacked me," Randy argued.

"Good, sounds like we can add public intoxication to the list of growing charges," Carter said, leading him away.

"I saw him," April said, watching them go. Her voice held a mix of fear and something else Jerry couldn't put his finger on.

"Don't worry about Randy. He's going away for a long time and won't be a threat to either you or Max now," Jerry said. A part of him thought the takedown was too easy and wished he'd been able to get in a lick or two, but the important thing was that April and Max were now safe.

"No, I'm saying Randy was right. It was Gunter! I saw him." April said, stepping outside and looking around.

Jerry smiled a wide smile. "You saw Gunter?"

"I did! The way he sailed through the air was amazing. He's so beautiful! I knew he would be because you say he looks like Houdini, but wow." April gasped. "Does that mean I can see ghosts?"

Jerry didn't want to burst her bubble, but the truth of the situation was that Gunter was standing directly in front of her, holding a cannoli between his teeth. That she couldn't see him now meant the spirit probably allowed her to see him to show her he would keep her safe. It was his vow to her. Gunter nudged him, and Jerry knew it was the dog's way of telling him it was his turn to make a vow to her.

Jerry took April by the hand, led her to the miniature bridge, and dropped to his knee. Though he'd practiced this moment for months, all the flowery things he'd wanted to say were lost. He pulled the box from his pocket and opened the lid to show her the ring. When he spoke, he spoke from his heart. "All my life, I've been running away from things and constantly searching for something to keep me grounded. That something is you. Now, instead of running away, I find myself wanting to run to you. I have never in my life felt so settled as I do when I'm with you. I love you and absolutely adore Max. Please say you'll marry me."

April nodded and smiled through a stream of tears. "After Randy, I never thought I would ever feel safe around another man. I built a wall around myself so that I could keep my daughter safe. That changed the day I met you."

"Is that a yes?" Jerry asked when she failed to say more.

"Of course it is." April's voice trembled when she spoke. "Yes, I'll marry you."

Jerry stood and pulled her into his arms.

Nearby, Purnell, Kris, and the others broke into a chorus of "I Love You Truly." Though April didn't appear to hear them, her eyes grew wide when Gunter joined in with a ghostly howl.

Coming Summer of 2024
Book 16 in The Jerry McNeal series
Hidden Treasures :
https://www.amazon.com/dp/B0D4L1RH46

Purchase autographed copies and series swag here:
www.dorrypress.com

About the Author

Sherry A. Burton writes in multiple genres and has won numerous awards for her books. Sherry's awards include the coveted Charles Loring Brace Award, for historical accuracy within her historical fiction series, The Orphan Train Saga. Sherry is a member of the National Orphan Train Society, presents lectures on the history of the orphan trains, and is listed on the NOTC Speaker's Bureau as an approved speaker.

Originally from Kentucky, Sherry and her Retired Navy Husband now call Michigan home. Sherry enjoys traveling and spending time with her husband of more than forty years.

Made in United States
Troutdale, OR
06/02/2024

20266313R10106